SUMMER

A novel by

LISA GRUNWALD

WARNER BOOKS

A Warner Communications Company

WARNER BOOKS EDITION

Grateful acknowledgment is made to Freddy Bienstock Enterprises
for permission to reprint an excerpt from "God Bless the Child"
by Billie Holiday and Arthur Herzog, Jr. Copyright © 1941.
Copyright renewed by Edward B. Marks Music Company. Used
by permission. All rights reserved.

Cover design by Jackie Merri Meyer
Cover illustration by Oren Sherman

This Warner Books Edition is published by arrangement with
Alfred A. Knopf Inc., subsidiary of Random House Inc., 201
E. 50th Street, New York, N.Y. 10022

Warner Books, Inc.
666 Fifth Avenue
New York, N.Y. 10103

A Warner Communications Company

Printed in the United States of America

First Warner Books Printing: July, 1987

10 9 8 7 6 5 4 3 2 1

Welcome to a 'SUMMER' you will never forget

"A STRUGGLE WITH THE POWER TO ENGAGE US. *Summer* draws an opposition between two kinds of art: art that celebrates life's power to change, and art that is man's attempt to control what he cannot."

—***New York Times Book Review***

* * *

"A STORY OF DEATH BECOMES A STORY OF LIFE.... What finally emerges and triumphs is the irresistible tug of life—the intricacies of love, the uplifting power of art, the challenge of growing and learning."

—***Booklist***

* * *

"A HEARTENING BOOK ABOUT LIFE'S MOST DISHEARTENING CALAMITIES... Lisa Grunwald's poignant first novel depicts death's 'terrible' encroachment as observed by Jennifer Burke, a college freshman whose unflappable mother suffers from a malignant spinal tumor... a perceptive commentary on the difficulty of relinquishing those we hold dear."

—***Philadelphia Inquirer***

* * *

"A HIGHLY ROMANTIC NOVEL... CARRIES A SOLID EMOTIONAL WALLOP."

—***People***

* * *

"POIGNANT AND UTTERLY BELIEVABLE... Grunwald makes us tremble for Jennifer and hope this family will survive. Jennifer is a character we care for... she is passionate, fumbling, and open-hearted. *Summer* moves swiftly... but should be read with care. In this first novel, every word counts."

—***San Francisco Chronicle***

* * *

"AN AFFECTING PORTRAIT OF LOSS."

—***Vanity Fair***

more...

* * *

"ADMIRABLY WELL-CRAFTED . . . *Summer* takes on real power when the narrator finally cracks into fury and grief, in taut scenes in which she, the daughter, must become the parent to her dying mother."

—*Newsweek*

* * *

"A BOOK ABOUT COMING OF AGE . . . perceptive . . . her characters are believable."

—*Baltimore Sun*

* * *

"A MOVING STORY . . . INSIGHTS THAT TELLINGLY TOUCH READERS' CHORDS."

—*Forbes*

* * *

"LISA GRUNWALD'S IS A NAME TO REMEMBER. . . . A sensitive hand and a delicate sensibility are at work in this poignant first novel . . . a touching story, haunting in its recognition of impending tragedy."

—*John Barkham Reviews*

For Toots and Hank

"Mother, give me the sun."

—HENRIK IBSEN,
Ghosts

JUNE

1

I don't remember the first question I asked my mother, or the last answer she gave me. But I do know the basics: "Why" from me, and "Just because" from her. "Why" is still one of my biggest pitfalls. Even close friends accuse me of thinking too much. But "Just because" was my mother's strong suit. She was better than anyone I've ever known at making those words work. She had no patience for brooding or misery because she herself could find pleasure anywhere: in a sunny day, in a rainy day, in a good fresh peach. My mother would say "Just because" to me, and it meant, "Relax, Jennifer. It's not worth worrying about. Let's have a peach."

Her name was Katherine, but in the family we called her Lulu. My older sister Hillary came up with the name. Hillary was always giving us nicknames, but "Lulu" was the one that stuck. I never thought of my mother as Katherine, and only rarely as Mother or Mom. She was Lulu. She was Lulu because of a certain, almost noble contentedness that she had about things. She was Lulu because of the way her shoulders went back and her chin went forward when she knew she was right. She was Lulu because she always knew she was right, because she usually was, and because when she wasn't she let us tease her mercilessly. She was the unshakable center of our lives.

She was born in Boston, the younger of two daughters in a very proper Back Bay home. Her family, Daddy once told me, had practically settled Boston. They'd all attended Harvard. The motto on their family crest was "Patience, Love and Dread." Daddy had grown up in Boston too, but his family was Irish and working class. They didn't have a crest.

My parents first met in New York City, when Lulu was down for the weekend from Radcliffe and Daddy was just starting to sculpt. That much I know has got to be true. The rest is romance, and anyone's guess. But the story went that Daddy had first seen Lulu at the Metropolitan Museum of Art—by Rodin's *Kiss,* no less. He had followed her to Dali's watches, Picasso's musicians and finally to Turner's seascapes, where he'd asked her out for coffee. After coffee he'd talked her into dinner, then lunch the next day, then another weekend. He talked her into posing for his sculptures and finally, after six months, into transferring to Barnard.

It wasn't a bad little story.

But when Lulu's father found out that she was modeling for Daddy—nude, of course—it was one terse telegram: PACK STOP COME HOME STOP. Lulu had neither gone home nor stopped. She and Daddy were married when Lulu was twenty and Daddy was twenty-three. That was the same year that Joe Pillari discovered him and gave him a one-man show; it was the year that his first sculpture was bought by the Whitney. But Lulu's parents were not impressed. They neatly disowned her, and she never looked back. Her parents were the two photographs that were hidden in her sewing box.

Lulu and Daddy lived in Greenwich Village during the early fifties. Daddy free-lanced for ad firms and did his sculpture in the evenings. Lulu spent her days sketching and painting, her nights as Daddy's model. Then they moved back to Boston and had Hillary and me, five years apart. Lulu gave up her painting but continued to pose for Daddy.

There is a sketch that he did of her around the time they first met. It was meant to have been just a study for a sculpture, but Daddy had gone back with charcoal and pastels to fill her features in. Lulu looks out from this drawing—eager, loving, preposterously strong—exactly as she was in all Daddy's sculptures, exactly as she seemed all my life. She had already made her choice then. She had traded her likenesses to him—her own impulsiveness, talent, selfishness, doubt—for the pleasure of their differences, which she helped to create. She had chosen to be his opposite: the pragmatist, the optimist, the anchor, the presence. It was impossible to imagine his success without her. It was impossible to imagine her contentment without that role. My parents formed a unit, inevitable and pure: the artist and his model, the wife and her husband, the father and mother, Lulu and Daddy, Milo and Katherine Burke.

Daddy was small and wiry and fast, with bright blue Irish eyes and curly brown hair. Lulu was tall and strong and blond. Daddy floated and puttered, intimidated and taught. He smiled when he carved a smiling face and frowned when he carved a sad one. Lulu raised her chin and threw her shoulders back and put her face into the sun. Hillary and I imagined their perfection the way most children imagine their parents' faults.

I took a photograph of them when I was fourteen and I was just starting to take pictures. It was black-and-white, as all my photographs were then, and it showed Lulu and Daddy wading out of the ocean at dusk. When I really stop to think of my parents, I always see them as they were in that photograph. The sky and sea blended into each other, the exact same shade of gray. Lulu and Daddy were in silhouette, Lulu in front with her hands on her hips, and Daddy behind her with his arms at his sides for balance. Between them were several clear points of white light, which was the sun reflected in the wake of Lulu's step. The lights made a line between them, like a rope with bright white buoys.

Some children grow up with a lot and assume they'll always have it. I grew up knowing I would lose it, although I don't know why ("Just because," Lulu would say). I stored up my memories like ammunition. I waited for changes. So when Lulu got cancer at the end of my freshman year, there was a part of me that was ready, a part of me that had already heard the tone of Daddy's voice as he told me the news on the telephone. There was also a part of me that was not ready, because for all the thinking I had done about their dying, it had never occurred to me that they wouldn't die together.

I was eighteen then, and I sat up for a long night in a noisy college dorm. It was the end of May. It was supposed to be the summer that my first book of photographs came out. Instead, I thought, it would be the summer I watched my mother die.

I listened to the laughter of my roommates in the living room. I tried to imagine Daddy without Lulu. I tried for hours and hours to imagine the black-and-white photograph without her in it. All I could see was the page torn in half, with the white fuzz of the mat board ruining the gray. I knew that he would not be able to live without her, and that night I decided that he wouldn't have to try.

I wanted them to die together for the same reason I take pictures: to freeze time, to preserve things as they are.

2

Our summers always began in the air. Somewhere between Boston and the Cape, Daddy always got silly and Lulu always started to talk about her rabbits. The rabbits were Lulu's nemesis. They ate all the flowers that she grew in her garden, and she always complained but never had the heart to do anything about them.

It was June 3, a Saturday. I flew in from Chicago and took a cab to Hanscom Field, a small airport near Boston where Daddy kept his plane. In my bag was a black leather portfolio filled with the photographs I'd taken in my year away at school.

I paid my fare and looked up to see my parents in the distance. Dying, I thought. The word evoked no image beyond the torn gray photograph.

Daddy was leaning against the old Piper. Lulu was sitting on the wing, her knees up, her hands on her ankles, her fine blond hair blown by the wind. I wanted to run to them. I felt like a child in a carnival crowd.

"You look terrific!" Daddy shouted when he saw me walking toward them. I forced a smile and hugged him.

"My turn," Lulu said. She hopped off the wing. She put her arms around me and whispered that she'd missed me. "I'm glad you're home," she said. I was awkward, and oddly embarrassed.

"How do you feel?" I asked her.

"Fine," she said, and the word dismissed the question. I looked at Daddy, but he was smiling.

"Where's Hillary?" I asked.

"Still in town," Lulu said. "She's got an audition Tuesday."

"For what?" I asked.

"A toothpaste commercial."

I laughed. "Why didn't she come for the weekend at least?"

Lulu looked at me with mock gravity. "Preparation," she said.

"For toothpaste? What does she have to do?"

"Floss," Daddy said.

Nothing was different. Nothing was going to be. Daddy was doing his absentminded professor routine ("We'll put these boxes up front . . . no, these . . . if you take the bags and I take the boxes . . ."), and Lulu was counting suitcases and checking things off on her inevitable list. Sanders Island, where we summered, lay six hours by boat off the coast of Cape Cod, and Lulu always packed for us as though we were on safari.

"Lulu," Daddy told me, peering over his horn-rimmed half-glasses, "is being the grown-up today."

Lulu and I climbed into the back seats, and Daddy put a few last bags in front.

"I wish it wasn't raining," I said.

"It's good for the lawn," Lulu said. "And the flowers. Maybe it'll keep the bunnies away."

"Did they say thunder, Daddy?"

He didn't turn around. He was finishing his preflight.

"Yes," he said, fiddling with some knobs and switches in front. "The largest thunderstorm that has ever swept the eastern seaboard. It's mania to be up here at all."

"Thank you."

"You're quite welcome."

"Anyway," Lulu said, "it'll all blow over."

I kissed her cheek. Lulu was always saying things would blow over. She said a lot of things like that: it'll all blow over; just because; you never know; make up your mind to change; anything is possible; the sooner you start the sooner you'll finish; do something right or don't do it at all. There were also more specific ones: don't walk barefoot or you'll catch a cold; a good cook always cleans up after herself; if you watch a scary movie you'll have nightmares till you're twenty-one. She believed them all, and for a long time I did too.

I put my head against her shoulder and my hand around the crook in her arm. I stayed that way as we took off and I felt the Piper straining into the air. There was the old smell of shampoo and cigarettes, and I knew that she wasn't going to die. She stroked my hair. She said how good it was to have me home and, again, how much she had missed me. I tried to imagine how fragile she was.

We'd been in the air only a few minutes when Daddy turned around with glee. He let go of the yoke and waved his arms.

"Hey, Jennifer," he said. "Who's going to fly the plane?"

"I've missed you, Dad," I said.

He laughed—he had a wonderful, fast, deep laugh that made me happy—and he switched on the automatic pilot. He reached into his jacket pocket for his carving. Everywhere Daddy went he took a block of wood and a penknife. It used to drive Lulu wild, because sometimes he would start to whittle in the middle of a fancy party. "Reality," she would say about him, "simply never intrudes."

She was looking out her window, past the drizzle misting the glass, and she was smoking a cigarette. I watched the worn suede arm of Daddy's jacket moving up and down. It was his favorite jacket, and I smiled realizing that Lulu hadn't yet convinced him to throw it out. She used to threaten to sew up the sleeves when he wasn't in it.

Pretty soon, the wood shavings started bouncing back under Daddy's seat.

"What's it going to be?" I shouted to him, leaning forward.

"It hasn't made up its mind yet."

I sat back, tapped Lulu's shoulder and pointed to the pile of shavings at our feet.

"Not a well man," she said.

Then the plane jerked and dropped. I gripped Lulu's hand. The drizzle turned into a downpour. Out the window there was a blanket of large motionless clouds. I knew we were moving, but I had no sense of motion. There was nothing to judge our speed by. I felt as if we were in a box suspended on a string. The plane began to shake. I felt sick. Rain was streaming down the windows and pounding on the roof of the plane. Lulu kissed my forehead and put her arm around me.

"Milo?" she shouted. "Can't you do anything?"

"Sorry, kid," he shouted back. They called each other kid. "Just look at the instruments, Jennifer."

He had thrown his knife and the carving onto the luggage as soon as we'd hit the weather. I could see that the carving was going to be a horse. I didn't look at the instruments. That never helped. What helped was looking at Daddy's hands. For as long as I could remember, Daddy's hands had been doing something: whittling, or drumming against a tabletop, or pushing his eyeglasses up on his nose.

I scrunched down tighter against Lulu, as if she could stop the rain.

"Where are the tops?" Daddy was saying into his headset. Tops are the tops of clouds. He was trying to find out if we could go higher and avoid all the bumps, but the controller must have said that the tops were too high.

"Sorry, darling," Daddy called back to me.

I closed my eyes. I waited for the shaking to stop. I gripped the armrest. Dying, I thought, and she's put my head against her shoulder.

"I'm going to go lower," Daddy finally said, and then I did look at the altimeter in the cockpit, with its thick white arms like clock hands moving too fast, and backwards. Three thousand to two thousand feet.

"It's all right, Jen," Lulu whispered to me. "It's going to be all right."

"Okay back there?" Daddy asked.

"We're fine," Lulu said, and I knew she was smiling at Daddy over my head.

About ten minutes later the clouds broke and the sun began to shine. The shaking stopped. We were moving again. I could see the island. From the air it looks like a crescent moon, and it was there, beneath us, like a page from my grade-school atlas: green, blue, beige. Once, over farmland when we all flew out west, I had told Lulu that the ground looked like a Mondrian painting without the black lines, and she had been proud of me for knowing about Mondrian.

I straightened up.

"I'm sorry," I said. I reached into Lulu's purse for a cigarette.

"That's my girl," she said.

I put my forehead against the window. The glass was buzzing, and it hurt my head, but I wanted to feel the sun on my face. Lulu was looking out her own window, and we circled the island, about to land. I watched Daddy's lips move as he spoke again over the radio, but I couldn't hear what he was saying. I watched his fingers drumming lightly on the yoke.

3

When we landed it was a little after four. Already the sun was stretching T-shaped shadows beneath the tail ends of the planes. Daddy tied the Piper down and took the bags out, then reached back into the cockpit for his wood and his knife.

"Whittle while you walk," he said, and went to get the old VW wagon from the airport garage.

Lulu and I sat with the bags in the sun on the airport benches. They were blue that year. Every year the Board of Selectmen allocated a certain amount of money to paint the benches a different color. The paint came out now in a bumpy texture like stucco, there were so many coats underneath.

"Did you bring the new pictures?" Lulu asked.

I hesitated. "Yes," I said.

"When do we get to see them?"

"Do you want to?"

"What do *you* think?"

A small red plane took off from the runway near us, and I

waited for the noise to fade, trying to phrase my question. But Lulu spoke up first.

"How'd you do for the term?" she asked.

"Professor Katzmeier gave me an A."

"Oh, Jen," she said, turning to face me.

"He said they were better than my book."

"He liked them?"

"He loved them."

"Wait till Milo hears," she said.

"Not till I show him."

"All right."

"Promise."

"All right."

She squeezed my hand. "I'm very proud of you," she said.

Everything was wrong.

"Are you tired?" I asked.

"A little."

"Does your back hurt?"

"A little."

"You're not going to talk about it, are you?"

"What's to say?"

4

Our house on Sanders was built high on a bluff on the inner rim of the island's crescent, about halfway between its two tips. Twenty feet below it was the beach, and you could only get to it by a wooden staircase, narrow and steep. Every winter the storms would wash the staircase away. Every summer Daddy would build a new one.

Lulu told us that when they bought the house, the beach was much sandier, and wider too. The jetty in front was meant to keep it that way, but it hadn't really helped. The beach grew narrower each year, and cluttered with rocks. Daddy took this personally. He would walk out to the porch at sunset, a drink shining in his hand like a scepter. He'd say, "Damned beach is shrinking. Pretty soon we won't need the staircase to go for a swim. We'll just dive straight off the porch."

So every summer he drew the beach from the same spot on the porch. The shrinking kingdom. On paper. Lulu framed every one of his beach drawings. They hung on the fireplace wall: nineteen identical frames, nineteen different changes. He always used charcoal when he was worried about something, or in a dry spell with his sculpture. He used pastels when things were going well. There were a lot of pastels. But I liked the earliest drawings the best. They were simple outlines, contour drawings, a life that was waiting to be colored in.

Hillary used to tease Daddy about his drawings. She'd say, "We *know* what it looks like, Dad." (Hillary could be a real charmer.) My approach to them was, typically, morbid. One day I figured out that there was room for only two more sketches on the wall where they hung, and I took that as a sign that Daddy would only be around long enough to *do* two more sketches.

I said to Lulu: "Maybe it means just two more years."

She laughed—she could never see things like that—and she said, "Don't be silly, Jen. We'll just rearrange them when the time comes. There'll be plenty of room. Bring your laundry downstairs." And I remember thinking she was brave but blind.

So I began my own recording of change. I spent one whole summer compiling a photo album of the best pictures that Daddy had taken of Lulu. I gave it to her on her birthday in August, and every summer after that I added a portrait to it. The book sat on one of the side tables near the fireplace, underneath Daddy's sketches.

The rest of our living room was like a huge glass box, with sliding doors that opened onto the porch. It was an artist's house. There were always coffee mugs and glasses on the counters and tables that were filled with bouquets of colored pens and pencils. Lulu used them to illustrate shopping lists (drawing a carton of milk instead of writing the word) and sometimes the menus for dinner. She would outline her sketches with a thick black marker and then fill them in with bright splashes of color. There was also a blackboard in the kitchen, where Daddy would leave drawings of flowers for Lulu, and messages and "cautionary drawings" for Hillary and me. My notion of punishment began with a chalkboard sketch of a girl sitting in her room alone.

The kitchen was the best part of the house. It had a large, free-standing fireplace with a high brick hearth that made a wonderful seat. It had great big baskets, copper pots, antique tins and wooden cabinets. Especially on Sanders, where Lulu had never hired a maid or a cook, she liked to have her things just so. She and Hillary always prepared food as if it were going to be photographed by some magazine.

Upstairs were Hillary's and my bedrooms. We also had sliding doors and porches. Mine looked out on the garden, and Hillary's on the ocean. There was an attic, too, with a staircase in the hall. Hillary had a trapdoor in her closet that led to it. Which wasn't fair, I had always said, because she wasn't the attic type. Once—once!—when I was ten and she was apologizing for some fight, she let me sleep in her room. It was the grandest possible gesture. But she woke me up halfway through the night and made me go back to my bed. I can still make her squirm a little if I remind her of that.

Lulu and Daddy's bedroom was downstairs. It was vast, with different levels and lots of molding and corners. It had big exposed beams in the ceiling and a blanket on the bed that Lulu had crocheted for them one winter. On Sundays, Hillary and I would bring the papers in, and the four of us would read and talk, Lulu and Daddy still under the covers, the two of us nestled between them or lying at their feet. That bed was the family meeting place.

There were also two spindled rocking chairs by the window that looked out on the ocean. There were two matching antique dressers that Lulu had found on one of her summer forays to the mainland. And there was an old rolltop desk where she did the bills and made appointments and kept all her catalogues and letters and slides. Lulu had started a folk art gallery on Boylston Street when Hillary went to college; her two middle-aged gay assistants (whom Lulu called The Boys) were always sending her things.

The desk was her command post, the place where she stashed the crucial supplies like Scotch tape and scissors, stapler and glue. Everything had its place, and Lulu and Daddy did too. Lulu's was at that desk or in the garden or kitchen, keeping order. Daddy's was wherever he could get the most work done.

5

Daddy was in the living room by the table at the window. I went in to watch the sunset with him. He was staring at the ocean. The sunlight fell on the dark wood walls in deep red patches. I stood beside him, nearly as tall. We could hear Lulu fussing in the kitchen and humming something off key. We could smell dinner cooking.

"In the plane today—" I began.

"I know. You were scared. My intrepid flier," he said, turning to face me.

"It wasn't that. It was Lulu," I said.

"*She* was okay."

"I know."

"What, then?"

"She was just the same. So were you. I didn't expect that."

Daddy looked back to the ocean and took off his glasses, rubbing his eyes.

"She wants to see my portfolio," I said.

"Well, so do I."

"It feels so strange."

"I know."

"She was taking care of me today," I said. "And I just let her. Shouldn't I be taking care of her?"

"I don't know, darling."

"What do you mean, you don't know?"

"I don't know."

"You're not supposed to say that," I said. He smiled at me faintly, then put his glasses on again. "I hate it when you say that," I whispered, smiling back.

He told me what he hadn't on the telephone: all the facts I didn't really want to know and that I found too specific, too real, coming from him. My father was a brilliant artist and the most loving man I've known, but he did not remember birthdays. He did not know how to balance a checkbook. Now he was standing by this sunlit ocean, using words I didn't know, telling me that the tumor on Lulu's spine was large and that she was being treated with chemotherapy and radiation. He said we would probably have to make at least one trip to Boston for the radiation, but that there was a doctor at the Sanders Medical Center (the island was too small to have a full-fledged hospital) who would be able to check up on her. Daddy got even more detailed, describing the drugs and the treatment. As the summer wore on, we would all become experts.

"She hasn't told anyone," he said quietly. "None of our friends know. She doesn't want them to."

"Figures," I said.

I looked at the ocean, with the cool blue waves, and the sun now behind the horizon.

"Do you know about *Neptune's Horses*?" Daddy asked.

"What?"

"*Neptune's Horses*. It's a painting by Walter Crane."

I made a mental search of all the works I'd studied in

classes, all the slides I'd seen in lectures and all the shelves at home in Boston, with their glossy rows of artist-name books.

"I've never seen it," I said. I braced myself for a quick, tough lecture about the importance of Walter Crane. But Daddy just pointed out the window.

"Look at the ocean," he instructed me. "The painting showed twelve white horses bearing Neptune, the god of the sea, to shore. See, the horses' manes were the crests of the waves. And their hooves were webbed, like ducks' feet. And their necks were arched to make the curves of the waves. It was fabulous. And all the foam, the whitecaps, were other horses' manes."

"What does this have to do with Lulu?" I asked.

His hands dropped by his sides.

"Why were you carving a horse today, Daddy?"

He smiled, his eyes merry, not mournful.

"That's my secret," he said.

6

Later that night Lulu and Daddy played chess. Chess was a summer ritual—like Daddy with the staircase or his sketches of the shoreline; like their evening swims at sunset and my photographs of Lulu. Nearly every night after dinner, Lulu and Daddy would settle down at the living room table and play a game, sometimes two. Daddy had made the set for them years before from some leftover marble. The pieces were about four times the usual height, with the neck of each figure stretched out, a lot like Daddy's real sculptures. The kings looked like Daddy and the queens like Lulu. The marble was smooth and heavy, and wonderful to touch.

Lulu and Daddy playing chess—I wish I'd actually taken that picture, but I never really needed to: Lulu's elbows on the table, and her chin resting in her hand, Daddy whittling or sketching or just watching the hourglass as he waited for her to move. When it was Daddy's turn he crossed his arms and leaned way back in his chair. Then Lulu would crochet or do needlepoint, and sometimes, surreptitiously, she would glance at her reflection in the window.

I don't know if they were any good, but they were certainly evenly matched. They always kept a season score well, and at the end of the summer they were never more than two or three games apart.

I did the dishes while they played, hearing over the running water the occasional laughter and the low, familiar voices. I thought of calling Hillary to talk things out, but figured I'd wait until she came. I thought about Jim Franks, a beautiful blond runner I had a terrible crush on. I wondered if he would call me or if I should call him. And I thought about my photographs, still tucked inside my suitcase. I needed a day in the darkroom, and then I'd be ready.

Lulu walked into the kitchen looking for an ashtray, her sandals clicking against the tiles with that always determined step.

"Who's winning?" I asked.

"I am," she said gaily, "but he thinks he is."

Later that night, I went downstairs for some milk, and I saw that they'd started a new season score. Lulu had won the first game. In the window I saw my own reflection—Lulu without the height or assurance—and walked outside to avoid it. I stared instead at the ocean. There was moonlight on the water, and I could just imagine Lulu and Daddy wading out onto the shore like ghosts.

7

When I woke the next morning, it couldn't have been any later than seven o'clock, but Lulu was already out in her garden.

"Look what they've done!" she was shouting at the lawn. "I'll kill 'em! I'll kill 'em!"

"They," of course, were the rabbits.

I slid the glass door open and walked out onto my porch. She was wearing a faded blue bathing suit underneath an old pair of Daddy's khaki shorts. She had twisted her hair into a bun that had already started to fall. Her back and her arms were pale, and there was a large bruise where the doctors had taken blood. It was the first sign I'd seen of her illness.

But otherwise she looked great. She had long thin legs that I didn't quite inherit and short strong hands that I think I did. She had the broadest, most elegant shoulders I've ever seen. Her shoulders and her back always got very tan and freckled in the sun, from bending into the garden.

Daddy was just the opposite—a great tan on his face, and his back as pale as marble.

"Good morning!" I called down. Lulu didn't look up.

"Hah!" she said.

"Oh, Lulu."

"Don't Lulu me. Look at them!" she cried fiercely, squinting up at me and pointing to the lawn. There was just the slightest trace of a smile on her face.

Two of the rabbits crept out from the bushes, hopping nimbly over the small wooden fence she had built to keep them out.

"They've come back for more! They have no shame!" She spun back to the lawn, scattering them with a wave of her trowel. "You have no shame!" she shouted.

"Is there coffee?" I asked.

"Not yet."

"How'd you sleep?"

"Fine."

"How do you feel?"

"Fine."

She looked up at me again. "Come down here, baby. It's going to be a beautiful day. Get some rocks and kill the bunnies like a good girl."

"It's too early to kill bunnies."

"They ate my zinnias."

"I'll make the coffee."

"Look at these weeds," she said. As I closed the door I heard her asking, "Why don't you guys like weeds?"

I went downstairs and made the coffee. Lulu walked in a few moments later.

"Let's get this place shipshape," she said.

"Lulu," I groaned. I was still half asleep.

She walked past me to the kitchen sink and started to wash her hands. "We've got to put fresh sheets on the beds and do the towels and the dishes," she said. "You never know what little critters have been around. There's a stack of old newspapers I want thrown out—"

Daddy ambled in, wearing his oldest blue jeans and a red flannel shirt.

"Good morning, beautiful women," he said, pulling a coffee mug down from the shelf. He turned to Lulu. "We've met before," he said.

"How'd you like a nice big steak tonight?" she asked.

"Why not?"

He poured a cup of coffee and took a first sip. "Who *made* this?" he asked.

"I did," I said.

"Your future is not in this kitchen." He kissed Lulu on the cheek. "I'm going to check the staircase damage," he said.

"Want me to make a fresh pot?" Lulu asked.

"Don't bother," he said. "Are you *sure* we haven't met before?"

"You must have me confused with someone else," she said.

He winked at me and walked out onto the porch.

"Let's get cracking," Lulu said.

"Do you realize it's only seven thirty?"

"The sooner you start the sooner you'll finish."

"Can I ask Daddy to help me?"

"Don't be silly. I'm going to help you."

"Shouldn't you be resting?"

"No." She almost shouted the word.

A half hour later, after I'd showered and changed and come back downstairs, I saw a fresh pot of coffee brewing for him on the stove.

8

Once when we were little and Hillary was sick, Daddy carved her a marionette. He used some spare wood from a sculpture, and the string Lulu kept in the kitchen for roasts. Daddy used bright colors to paint it. Its face was smiling and silly. I remember its eyes were green. Hillary named it Cleo. I was jealous. I wanted one too.

On my birthday a few months later, Daddy came through with another marionette. The strings on this one were delicate fibers. The crosspiece was smooth and even. They were another tradition, the marionettes. Each birthday brought a new one. They were splendid, funny, hard to describe: real creatures that we had only to name.

In the summers we put on puppet shows. Hillary took all the best parts, and I think that's when she began her acting. I preferred to help Lulu with the scenery. Daddy put up a stage in the woods by an inlet we named the puppet pond. Every few summers Lulu would make new curtains. We kept the marionettes in a large wicker trunk that I hated to close on them.

The puppets were the source of the only argument I heard my parents have. It happened when I was ten. We had just done a show, and the four of us were walking home through the woods.

"They're wonderful," Lulu had said to Daddy.

"Thank you," he'd answered, smiling.

"They come straight from you, Milo, you know. They *are* you. The best part of you."

"Maybe." His smile, I remember, had faded a bit.

"Why can't your real art be like that?"

"Kid," he had said, still trying to be light, "you're tired of posing for me."

"No. I'm serious," she'd said. I had reached out a hand for Hillary, scared. "Why can't your real art be like that? Colors? And funny? Why not?" she had asked.

"Because it *is* real art," he had said.

That was it. That was their argument. They had it many times. They never yelled. They never let that argument create other arguments—at least none that I knew about. But it was always there. It was the one thing they simply couldn't agree on, though I think it scared them less than it scared Hillary and me.

We put the puppets in the trunk that day, figuring they were the problem. But the argument went on. Whenever Daddy worried about getting into a rut with his sculpture, Lulu would raise a meaningful eyebrow. Whenever a faddish new sculpture was shot down by the critics, Daddy would tape the review to the blackboard in the kitchen.

Daddy stopped adding to our collection. We didn't play with the puppets again. The stage we had built stayed in the woods and weathered. The curtains were rained on and torn, and finally they disappeared completely, leaving only the wide wooden frame from which they had hung.

9

"The studio," Lulu said to me as she pulled a dark green crewneck sweater over her head. Lulu looked great in dark green. I was lying at the foot of her bed, leafing through a catalogue that one of The Boys had sent her. She was standing in front of the mirror, putting on her lipstick.

"Oh, Lulu," I said.

It was Monday. We had spent all Sunday cleaning the house. Now Lulu and Daddy were getting ready to go see Bob Reese. Bob was a Sanders hermit, an artist who painted only the ocean, but painted it very well. Lulu had discovered him. She had convinced Joe Pillari to give him a wall in one of his group shows in SoHo, and that had been Bob's great, if late, start. Bob was the closest thing my parents had to a friend. Everyone else was an acquaintance, an associate or an intrusion on the family.

"It needs to be done," Lulu said.

"Can't he do it?"

"Don't be silly."

"I want to work on my own prints," I said. "I want to show you and Daddy."

"Later. After you finish the studio." She turned to face me, perfectly posed, her shoulders thrown back. "How do I look?"

"You look great," I said.

"We won't be long. Give me a kiss."

I stood up and kissed her. Then I was sorry I had complained about the studio.

It was noon when Lulu and Daddy drove off. I lay on their bed, finding faces in the knotholes of the wooden ceiling. I waited until I couldn't hear the car any more. Then I went to the kitchen and made some hot chocolate.

I walked across the deck to the studio. Daddy's studio was just called a studio. It was really the house's original garage, which Lulu had converted for him one summer. She had painted the walls and the ceiling and the floor white, and then she had had large picture windows installed, like the ones in the main house. The windows were a mistake. At night, all the moths thumped against the glass, and in the daytime, when the wind blew up from the ocean, the windows fogged and rattled.

I put my cocoa on the deck and reached into the drainpipe gutter for the key. The lock was rusty, and the door had swollen with the winter's storms. I tugged and tugged and finally pulled it open, knocking the cocoa over with my foot. It ran along the splinters of the wood.

I was always Daddy's daughter when I entered his studio. It was the place of our long talks, the place of his imagination and my ambition. Now I entered as Lulu's daughter, with a broom in my hand and the job of making order.

Daddy had covered everything with white sheets. Beyond the foggy windows were the sand and the sea grass. The drop cloths looked like a part of the landscape: cotton sand dunes with a rise and fall. I stood and looked for a long time. Then I went upstairs to get my camera.

It took me hours to do, but I set up a series of shots, uncovering bits of old sculptures and floor and equipment as I pulled the sheets back. I imagined the photographs as a series, a montage, almost like a movie with a story to tell. The story was the uncovering. I still think Daddy's sculptures are the most beautiful sculptures in the world.

Parts of certain molds lay under the drop cloths: torsos, busts, legs. As I cleaned away the debris I uncovered these shapes and continued to photograph. It was probably the one time I managed, in however slight a way, to be both my parents at once. I knew that then. It was why I had brought my camera downstairs.

I was on my last frame when they pulled up in the VW. I watched from the window as Lulu sprang out of the car and strode into the house. Daddy, thinking that no one could see him, took off his glasses, ran his fingers through his hair, then put his head against his hands on the steering wheel. I never took the last frame in the series. I stared at my father.

The thing was that I could not imagine him driving up in a car without her. I could not imagine him waking up without her. I could not imagine his hand without its wedding ring, or who would buy his shirts or get his dinner ready or be his model or pack their bags or play chess with him or make him funny. Sitting there alone in the car, he looked small and old. Only a few moments before, he had looked elfin and happy.

He went inside too, and after a while I could hear them both calling hello to me. But I stayed in Daddy's studio, trying again to imagine the gray picture of them, the black shape of Daddy without the white sunlight before him, marking his way.

They needed to be together. They needed to stay together. It was not that I thought they would *always* be together if I ended their lives for them at the same time. I didn't believe in heaven. I didn't believe in anything. I only thought of death as a moment in a life, a moment I knew they had to share as surely as I knew their faces, their hands, their footsteps, the smell of her lipstick, the sound of his laughter late at night. If lives could be seen as dotted lines, and death the last marking, then their lines had to be exactly equal in length. Neither could extend beyond the other.

I wondered how to do it. I thought about it the way I think about taking pictures. It was a problem to solve, a solution to create. It was simply never a crime.

10

I spent the next day in my darkroom, a tiny shack in the back of Daddy's studio that I'd set up several summers before—with Lulu's help, of course. It was a small but sufficient place, and I kept it spotless. I loved the precision that photography demanded.

I had taken nearly every studio art class in high school. I had endured the hovering optimism of my teachers ("It's Milo Burke's daughter!") and the growing awareness on all our parts that what I had in name I definitely lacked in talent. I simply could not draw. I could handle a still life well enough, through sheer brute force perhaps, and I had a fair sense of color. But if someone said "Draw a cat" and didn't put a cat before me, I drew a fuzzy ball of nothing with some whiskers and a tail.

Photography was different. It supplied me with the cat and then let me go. It didn't make me start with a blank page. It produced memories but required none. I loved everything about it. I loved translating colors into black and white. I loved squeezing the world into one small rectangle, snapping the shutter and letting the world expand again.

I had just turned seventeen when one of Lulu's friends saw some of my prints and asked Lulu if he could take them to a publisher he knew in New York. Every time I called John Thomas's office I was told that the prints were "on his desk." I waited for months and months. I imagined a very large, very cluttered desk. Then I went to college. I signed up for photography classes and began, hesitantly, to take pictures in color. I got good grades. Finally, in March, a letter arrived from Thomas. How did I feel, the letter asked, about the title *Pictures at Dawn*?

I remember running across campus to find a telephone booth. I remember clutching the receiver in both hands as I talked to Lulu and Daddy. I remember seeing myself in the smudged metal face of the telephone and thinking, for once, that I really did look like Lulu. She and Daddy said they loved me and were proud of me and that I was really going to do it.

Now, alone in my darkroom, I swirled the new prints in the chemicals and shivered a bit with the memory of March. I wanted to make it happen again.

I worked through the afternoon. At around four I went to find them. They were standing together at the far end of the porch. They were laughing. Daddy had his arm around Lulu's waist. I wondered if he was acting. They were blond and brown from the back, light and dark, the perfect halves of each other.

The air was cool and the sun was strong, and I could still see Daddy's horses in the waves.

I walked into the living room. On the cocktail table were unemptied ashtrays, plates of cheese and crackers, a half-dozen empty glasses sheathed in damp napkins.

"Don't slouch like that," Lulu said, coming up behind me. "And give me a hand."

"I missed the party."

"It wasn't a real party," she said merrily. "Bob Reese just stopped by with some friends. Didn't you hear us?"

"No," I said. "I was working. Why didn't you call me? Was Daddy here?"

"Thank God. I can't *stand* Althea, you know."

"Big sis."

"She still treats him like a kid." Lulu laughed. "She treats everyone like a kid."

I followed her into the kitchen, carrying glasses.

"How'd the work go?" she finally asked.

I smiled at her and blushed a bit. "I'm ready," I said. "If you really want to see them."

"What do you *think*? I'll tell Daddy. Come on."

Out on the deck, Daddy was standing at the railing, staring off to sea.

"What's he going to be working on?" I whispered to Lulu.

"He hasn't told me yet."

"He was carving a horse in the plane."

"Really? That's funny."

"He's never done animals before, has he?"

"I don't think so."

"Are you going to pose for him still?"

"We'll see."

"But Lulu—"

"Come on," she said. "Let's tell him."

I held her arm for a moment.

"What's he thinking about?" I asked.

"Who ever knows?" she said, though of course I believed that she always did. "Come on," she said again. "Let's tell him."

It was only the first time that summer that I found myself wishing she could act more needy, less magnanimous somehow. Any way that would make the future more real. So as we walked together toward Daddy and she put her arms around him, I had my first glimpse of a truth that grew and grew as the weeks went by. Dying would not be something done in an instant, either with the expected roles or the expected emotions involved: half the hardness of it seemed to be knowing when it had begun.

11

Daddy's studio was still stuffy, even though the air outside had begun to cool. My photographs were stacked on his worktable. I sat on one of the sawhorses, and a large gray moth flew off toward the overhead light. Daddy shut the door behind him.

"You okay?" he asked me.

"Sure. Are you?"

He nodded, pulling his carving from his pocket with one hand as he patted my cheek with the other. He looked at me fondly, his eyes twinkling like evening lights.

"You didn't like them," I said.

But he didn't laugh. He scooped up his pocketknife from the worktable and sat on the second sawhorse. We had taken these seats many times before—whenever I had summoned the courage to try to understand him. What's composition, I had asked him here. What's negative space? How did you know that you loved Lulu? Did you ever love anyone else? When did you first want to be an artist? Do you believe in

God? Where did you find your own style? Why are there only three primary colors?

He had always been patient and simple, had always challenged me to ask more.

"Well?" was all I could ask him now.

He began to whittle. Wood shavings fluttered like dead leaves to the floor. I couldn't see his eyes.

"Well, the first thing," he began gently, "is that you know photography isn't my field, and the second is that I think you tried too hard this time."

"Too hard?"

I looked down, seeing the cracks between the floorboards where the white paint had dripped.

"I think you've gotten a little self-conscious."

"On which ones?"

He looked up from his carving.

"In general."

"Oh."

"You're not using your eye," he said firmly. "You've got an eye. I've told you that."

He had. They were the four words that had meant even more than I love you. Now they were an accusation.

Daddy put his carving down, his hands closing around an invisible shape. "You want to make people feel things when they see your pictures, right?"

"I guess," I said.

"Believe me, darling. That's what art's *for.*"

"But I got an A," I said, regretting it immediately.

"I don't think you should have."

"Daddy."

He shook his head. "I'm sorry. I'm sorry, Jen. I didn't mean it like that." He sighed and pushed his glasses up on his nose. "I'm sure your teachers know their subject. And I'm not saying the pictures are *bad*. God knows for an eighteen-year-old they're *worth* an A. It's just I know you're better than that."

"I'm sorry," I said.

He waved his arms. "You just *can't* make people *feel* things if you've got 'Feel Things' written over everything you do."

"I'm sorry," I said again, feeling my throat get knotty.

"Don't be sorry. You'll take more pictures. You'll take *better* pictures. You've got to."

"Don't get mad."

"I'm not getting mad. I'm excited. You know how I am. You've got an *eye*," he said again.

"I thought that you would like these." It was all I could say. I was trying not to cry. I was going to be an artist.

He stood up and took three steps toward me, cupping his hand around the back of my head. "Now, look, Jennifer," he said. "I've told you this before. I don't *know* photography. I can only tell you what I think. In the end you've got to trust yourself."

"I will," I mumbled.

"I'm crazy about you," he said, kissing my cheek.

"Thank you, Daddy."

I walked outside. Trust myself. He might as well have asked me to draw a cat.

I cried on the beach. I cried in the woods. I cried at the puppet pond. I cried all the way back to the house with the wind picking up, and then for about an hour in Lulu's arms. And when I finally couldn't cry any more, she said, "You know, Jen, I think you're taking this *very* well."

12

That night I lay in bed, seeing my photographs in my mind. The red-faced man with the bright white hair and the baby wrapped in the pink blanket. The black boys from the South End, their faces filling the page and only their white eyes defining them. The lady on the park bench with the pigeons around her. Yes, I thought, squirming, they were self-conscious. They were precious.

Professor Katzmeier fell from grace.

13

Hillary's plane was due in the next day. Sullen and sleepy, I got ready to leave for the airport. Daddy was helping Lulu weed in the garden, something I could not remember having seen him do before. I was surprised that he still hadn't started his work.

As I walked past them on my way to the car, I could hear Lulu humming "God Bless the Child"—off key, as usual. It was a song she'd heard me sing once, and she'd said she liked the words.

Daddy poked his head into the car just as I was about to start it up.

"Jen," he whispered so Lulu couldn't hear. "I hope I wasn't too hard on you last night."

"That's okay, Daddy."

"You know it's a tough time," he said.

"I know."

"It's just that you can do better."

"I will, Daddy," I said.

"I love you."

"I love you, too. Don't worry, Daddy. Really."

"Really?" He looked just like a boy.

I nodded.

"Well," he said, "I'm still sorry if I upset you." He glanced back at Lulu and then at me. "I guess my emotions are a little bit raw."

It was the first admission anyone had made, and I felt fiercely grateful.

14

The road to town was just a narrow dirt road, bumpy and curved. To the left of our house it wound along to the farthest tip of the island's crescent, where there was a long stone jetty that was gold and silver. To the right of our house, the road cut through the woods—past the old puppet stand, the puppet pond and the stream that led to it with a narrow wooden footbridge. Beyond the woods, our road fed into the island's main thoroughfare, Beach Street, which traced the outer arc of the crescent and led straight to the airport.

I liked to take the dirt road fast, and I liked to make a detour in town at the old Episcopal church. We were not a religious family. Lulu and Daddy associated religion with the very worst of Boston. But I loved the old church because each week it framed a quotation in its front window, sometimes biblical, usually not. The quotations always had an eerie way of applying to my life (I liked fortune cookies in those days, too).

But I didn't drive to the church that day. I thought about my father. I thought of his eyes, and his wonderful hands, and his laugh, and how hard he would have to try.

15

The Sanders airport terminal was not the island's garden spot. Its one long corridor was covered waist-high with bright green shag carpeting. On the walls were faded maps and aerial views of the island, and plaques for the Sanders pilots who had died in World War II.

I walked down the corridor past the rest rooms and the coffee shop to the radio room at the end of the hall. I looked for Harry, the airport manager, but he wasn't there. I bought a pack of cigarettes at the machine and lit one. Then I went into the coffee shop, but the girl at the counter said she hadn't seen Harry all day. I tried the charter desk and the car rental desk and then headed back to the radio room.

"Are you going to keep circling? Or are you going to land somewhere?"

I turned to see a tall, awkward boy leaning against Harry's desk with his hands in his pockets. I laughed.

"I was looking for Harry," I said.

"Harry's not here."

"Where is he?"

"He's sick," the boy said.

"Oh, no! Is he okay?"

"No. He's sick."

I laughed again. "I meant—"

"I know. No, it's nothing serious. Probably just drank too much last night. Can I help you out?" He walked around to Harry's chair and pulled it out from under the desk, nearly knocking it over. I laughed again, but was sorry I had. He glared at me defensively.

"I don't think so," I said quickly as I watched him sit down. "I'm trying to find out about my sister's plane. It's a charter. N-four-two-X-L."

"Nope. N-four-two-X-*M*," he said, clearly delighted with himself. "Close, though. It's twenty minutes late. Lots of traffic." He pointed vaguely out the window.

"How do you know these things?"

"I have my sources."

He flicked a few switches on one of the radios. As far as I could tell, they were strictly for show.

"Thanks," I said, and left.

Out on the runway, I stood by the old wooden split-rail fence, looking at the orange wind sock flapping in the distance, sickened a bit by the hot air around me and the smell of the fuel. Off on the field, mechanics and pilots were shouting and working over an old Beechcraft.

I watched the light planes taking off: bright colors and a pilot's face in shadow; the next moment a spot of color so easily lost, so far above everything, that it was indistinguishable from all the others. I realized what I was going to do. I was going to make Lulu and Daddy's plane go down.

It would be the end of the summer, I thought. Lulu would have to be flown off the island. She would be transferred from our car to the back seats in the plane. Daddy would climb into the cockpit. I'd lean into the cabin and kiss her good-bye. I'd say:

"See you tomorrow. Just as soon as Hillary and I close up the house."

Then I'd kiss Daddy good-bye and whisper: "Call us if anything happens."

Then I'd walk back to the blue bench with the stucco paint, and I would feel very brave and certain, and I would wait while the plane took off, and Daddy would never have to be alone and I would never see them again.

I was leaning against the fence and crying.

It would be the end of the summer.

How I would arrange it was a whole other problem. I knew nothing about how planes worked, and though Daddy had always wanted Hillary and me to learn to fly, we had always resisted. But I had found my solution. I knew it. It felt right.

I wiped my face with my sleeve. I looked around. I saw the boy from the radio room standing a few yards away by a bright yellow Cessna even smaller than Daddy's plane. He had a yellow rag in his hand. He cocked his head to one side, as if he were about to ask a question. But I turned back to the runway. Hillary's plane landed a few moments later.

"How is she?" she asked as she walked through the gate.

"She's fine."

"I mean really."

"Well, you know. She's being Lulu. She's acting like nothing's happening."

Hillary shrugged and reached into her bag for a comb. She ran it through her perfectly unmessed hair.

"Maybe nothing *is* happening," she said.

"How can you say that?"

She put her comb back in her purse and stared at me hard. She was tall like Lulu, and beautiful and blond like

Lulu. She had those same broad shoulders, strong chin and long legs. But there was nothing soft about her. We almost never touched.

"Have you heard something new?" she asked.

"No. Stop looking at me like that."

"Not everyone dies who has cancer. Maybe she won't let herself."

"I know it from looking at Daddy," I said.

We reached the car.

"Do you cry about it?" I asked her.

"Sometimes. In the tub."

16

"What do you see?"

Daddy asked the question for the first time when we were just little girls. It was a game he invented for the long drive down Beach Street. He told us to close our eyes—even Lulu—with our faces toward the window nearest the shore. You could always sense the sun, even when your eyes were closed, except if a house or a tree or something else stood in the way. Then the light would seem to get darker behind your eyes.

"What do you see?"

"Tree," one of us would shout, if the darkness lasted just a moment.

"Right," Daddy would say.

"Mansion," one of us would say.

"Wrong."

"Beach house."

"Right."

"Lighthouse."

"Right."

"Giant," Lulu said once.

"Lulu wins," Daddy had said.

The four of us played a lot of games together—Duck Duck Goose, Mother May I, Ring-Around-the-Rosie. It never occurred to parents or children that the games might have been more fun if there were more people playing and if the people were other children. Long before Hillary and I knew the word for them, we understood that even our friends were only acquaintances. We understood that what really counted happened only in the family. The four of us made up a shape that was as absolutely right as it was inescapable, though none of us would have dreamed of wanting to escape it then. The pieces of us simply fit, and fit tight: nothing, and no one, was allowed between us. It was always implied—and sometimes stated outright—that life was at its best when the doors were closed and we were alone. We never questioned Lulu's need to make the family an island. She and Daddy were best friends. Hillary and I were expected to be also.

It wasn't easy. Hillary and I were really total opposites. Recently I've come to think that we were each a side of Lulu: I more the inside, she more the outside. In Lulu, the two parts made a whole. Apart from Lulu, they made chaos. Hillary and I fought bitterly, competed fiercely. But we were also confederates, united by the same goal and the same frustration with it. Underneath all the stabs we made at each other, we knew that what we each wanted most was our parents' pride. It was all we ever cared about, our one truest addiction. But nothing was ever enough. We were never allowed to find a plateau that didn't become, in time, a forbidden retreat.

For all that—because of all that—we were closer than any two sisters I've known. When honesty won out over competition, we would sit on the staircase landing at night and talk for hours about men, or boys, and about Lulu and Daddy while they played chess below. We would recall parts of the story—how they had met, what they had looked like, how Daddy had proposed to her, how she had accepted. Like all sisters in close families, we had a private language and very few separate memories. We had always been with each other, and we were not allowed to pretend.

17

Daddy was working on the staircase when Hillary and I got home from the airport. He still hadn't started to sculpt. I wondered if Lulu would be able to pose for him. I wondered if he would ask Hillary or me instead. I walked upstairs, leaving Hillary and Lulu to chatter on the porch. It would be the end of the summer, I thought. We would have to transfer Lulu from the car to the plane.

In my room, on my bed, Daddy had left a sketch for me of the two of us. It was done in pastels and pencil. It showed us talking in his studio. Sunlight made a large triangle to the left of where we sat, out of the sun, away from the light. It was exquisite. It needed no note, and there was none. I still have it, framed and hanging on my wall.

Later that night Hillary and I sat up on the landing. I was cleaning my camera lenses, and we were smoking cigarettes. Lulu and Daddy were playing their second game of chess that night. Daddy had won the first, and Lulu had demanded a rematch.

"I've got to quit smoking," Hillary said, running a long, cool finger over the perfect fringe of her bangs. "I'm really going to get in shape this summer."

"You *are* in shape."

"That's all you know."

Nothing changes, I thought. Not even now.

"Tell me about Spencer," I said. That was her new boyfriend.

"Nothing much to tell."

"What do you mean?"

"Nothing to tell. He's just a guy."

"If he's just a guy, then why are you bringing him up here? Especially now?"

"Don't get nasty. It changes your face."

"Hills," I said. "Why now?"

She took a drag of her cigarette, blowing the smoke out in perfect rings. "To be honest, I don't know," she said. She waved the rings away as if each one had a diamond in it.

"Is this a contender?" I asked.

"*Contender.* You sound like Lulu. This is a fuck."

I winced, and she smiled, delighted. She loved to shock me, though God knows that wasn't much of a challenge in those days.

"Is that what you told Lulu?" I asked prudishly. "That Spencer is just a fuck?"

"Actually, she didn't ask."

"Why'd you get involved with him?"

Hillary smiled and examined the tiny red band of lipstick on her cigarette.

"It's silly," she said coquettishly. "He asked me if I was going out with anyone, and I said, 'No, I'm sort of *between* lovers right now,' and *he* said, 'That sounds painful.' " She started laughing.

"Swell," I said.

"Oh, Jen, you're so old-fashioned."

I had finished with my lenses and started to put them back in the case.

"Look," she said. "Maybe part of it is that I thought having him around sometimes would keep us all from getting too intense."

"We *are* intense. We're *always* intense."

"Well, I don't think we should be now."

"Did you talk to Daddy?"

"Not yet. I can't face him."

"Neither can I."

"Has he been working?" she asked.

"No."

"What does Lulu say?"

"She hasn't said anything to me."

Hillary sighed. "Look, Jen," she said, "I think it's too soon to worry. Don't get everyone upset. This is one time where you cannot get into a lot of long metaphysical discussions."

"I know."

"Worry not."

"Worry not?"

"Shakespeare," she said. "I'm reading in August for *Romeo and Juliet*."

"So when do we worry?"

"Crisis time," she said, standing up. "I've thought about this. Really. The minute it's crisis time I'll send Spencer packing, and then you and I can fight it out to see who's braver."

18

I spent Thursday sunbathing, lying out on the wooden planks of the deck. Hillary sat nearby doing leg lifts and rehearsing the balcony scene.

"O, Romeo, Romeo! wherefore art thou, Romeo?"

"You've got it all wrong," I said.

"What do *you* know?"

"It's not 'wherefore *art* thou, Romeo.' It's '*wherefore* art thou Romeo.' "

"That's what I said."

"No. You said, 'wherefore *art* thou.' Wherefore doesn't mean where. It means why."

She stopped her leg lifts. "Really?"

"Really."

"How do you know this?"

"I have my sources," I said, and suddenly recalled the young pilot at Harry's desk. It would be the end of the summer. Lulu would have to be transferred from the back of the car. I would lean in to kiss her good-bye. "Now I hope you'll take this in the proper spirit,'' I said to Hillary. ''But if you don't stop rehearsing that speech I'm going to hurt you.''

She walked off down the porch. I closed my eyes. I could hear Daddy hammering away at the staircase on the beach, and the spritz of Lulu's lawn sprinkler. She would have to put her knees up a little, and we would have brought pillows for her. I would lean into the cabin and kiss her good-bye. I'd say:

''See you tomorrow, Mommy. Hillary and I will close up the house.''

She would say, ''Don't forget to close up the fireplace. Keep all the little critters from getting in.''

Then I'd kiss Daddy good-bye, and I'd whisper: ''Call us if anything happens. Even if you just want to talk.''

Then I'd wave good-bye and walk back to the blue bench with the stucco paint, and I'd wait while the plane took off. I would watch until it disappeared, and I would never see them again.

''Oh, Romeo, Romeo,'' Hillary was saying, her towel draped over one shoulder.

''Cut it out,'' I said. ''Or at least get off the first line.''

We could hear Lulu laughing with Sam in the garden. Sam was the handyman. He helped Lulu do whatever she didn't want to do or, in rarer cases, couldn't. Sam cleaned the leaves out of the drainpipes, carted up topsoil and loam for the garden, repainted the white railings and the fences. We used to accuse Lulu of inventing chores for Sam so he would have the added income. Sam was a lovable old islander with a back like a board. He always walked bent forward at a slight angle from the hip. His face was mossy and gray. He called Hillary and me ''Girl One'' and ''Girl Two,'' but interchangeably. He adored Lulu. He was always polite and deferential, but you could tell that she gave him a real kick. Sometimes, when her back was turned and she had just asked him to buy some more white paint, he would raise an eyebrow to me and point a finger at Lulu and wink.

Hillary and I stayed in the sun. At one point we went down to the beach and looked for Daddy, but he had finished the staircase and was gone. We went for a swim, diving off the jetty, racing to the buoy and back and arguing, as always, about who had touched the large rocks first.

"I want to photograph you," I said, when we had settled back down on the porch.

"Great."

"I knew I'd have to twist your arm."

"Well, I need a new portfolio."

"I need to learn how to take pictures again."

"Lulu told me what Daddy said."

"It wasn't a very good evening."

"When do we start?" she asked.

"As soon as you want to. How about now?"

"Don't be absurd. My hair's all wet."

"Tomorrow."

"I need to be more tan."

"It's black-and-white, Hills. Your tan won't show."

"I'll know it's there," she said—a very Lulu thing to say.

We lazed and drifted through the afternoon, and Daddy didn't return till dinner. He didn't say where he'd been, and no one had the nerve to ask.

19

The package was large and flat, and it was waiting in our mailbox at the end of the road the next afternoon.

"Lulu!" I shouted up the driveway to the lawn. "Lulu! It's the book!"

"Oh, Jen!"

I ran up the sandy pathway, tearing the brown paper away. I hadn't thought I'd be excited, but my heart was racing. *Pictures at Dawn,* it said, in thin white letters on gray. *By Jennifer Burke,* it said. I stopped running and let my hand glide over the cool, smooth cover. We had seen the galleys and seen the jacket, but this was very different.

"Bring it here!" Lulu shouted. "Milo!" she called as I started running again. "Milo! Quick!"

"Daddy!" I called.

"What is it?" Hillary asked, rushing out to the garden. She looked scared.

"My book, Hills, my book."

"Oh, is *that* all."

"Careful," Lulu said as Hillary took it from her hands. "Where's Daddy?"

"Don't know," Hillary answered, leafing through the pages.

We kept on calling him. We even went down to the beach. But it was hours and hours before he came back to the house. When we finally heard his footsteps coming up the stairs, the three of us had been through the book a dozen times, but we rushed to the railing of the house.

"Milo!" Lulu called down to him. "The book's here. It's here!"

He bounded up the stairs, and I was flushed and proud. We clustered around him as he took the book and sat at the picnic table. No one said a word as he opened it.

"Don't you think the title's silly?" I asked. "I still think it's kind of silly—"

"Hush," Lulu said. She looked up and met Daddy's eyes. She was smiling. My face felt hot and my hands were cold. It was just like March, except that I could see their faces.

"She's got an eye," Daddy said to Lulu.

"I'll start dinner," Hillary said. She left me a moment alone with them. It was a graceful gesture. There was more silence, then Lulu reached for me and embraced me, my face against her neck.

"I'm so proud of you," she whispered. Then she went to help with dinner.

Daddy and I sat out on the porch together, his hands darting from page to page and picture to picture while he asked questions, made comments, made suggestions about what I should try next. The wind picked up, and I was shivering. The prints got harder and harder to see. Daddy believed in my eye—in my ability to find surprises. He believed something about that ability that it took the whole summer for me to see. But his enthusiasm seemed to lift us both—over the house, the ocean, the illness.

"You've got to keep this going," he told me fiercely.

"I will, Daddy," I said. I still don't know if he ever understood the absolute mirror he was to me.

20

Upstairs, after the sun had set, I walked out to Hillary's porch and looked at the ocean. The waves were dark and calm, and I couldn't see Daddy's horses in them at all, but I did see Lulu and Daddy coming out of the water. They looked exactly as they did in my photograph: Lulu in front, Daddy behind her. Only the lights between them were missing. But the stars had come out. I thought about taking the picture again, but knew that I didn't have time. Then Lulu stumbled on a rock, and Daddy caught her. They stopped to kiss. Dying, I thought. Maybe she won't let herself, Hillary had said.

I heard Hillary's footsteps on the porch below.

"Hey, brat," she said.

We leaned over the railings and looked at each other.

"What," she asked, "are we going to do with these two?"

21

I started on Hillary's pictures Saturday. They were the last photographs I would take all summer, though I didn't know it then.

I dressed her in a black turtleneck, black shorts and black knee socks. I posed her on the deck, with her legs straddling the white railing and her hands behind her. It was a very sexy pose.

"Look at me," I said.

"You're taking too long. The wind's blowing."

"Quiet."

I started snapping. The wind blew her bangs into a side part, and I snapped one shot of her like that. She looked completely exasperated. As I took it I knew it would be the best, but I took a whole roll anyway. The shot with the wind turned out to be her favorite.

"Do another pose," she said.

"No. That's enough for one day."

As I put my cameras away, she pointed to Lulu and Daddy down the beach, as far away as a kite.

"Do you think they talk about it?" I asked.

"No way."

"Would you?"

"I don't know," she said.

"Has Daddy asked you to pose for him?"

"No. Has he asked you?"

"No. Do you think he's going to work at all?"

"He's got to," she said. "Lulu."

"I know. He told me when we got here that he had a secret," I said.

"Maybe it's another woman."

That made us both laugh.

22

I spent the night in the darkroom, imagining Daddy's happiness if the prints turned out well. In the morning I woke early. The sun was on my face. I had closed the window the night before to keep out the rain and the small gnats that came in through the screen when the wind blew from the east. Now the sun was hot through the glass. I reached up and opened the window, and a cool breeze floated in over the sunshine. I smiled and stretched and then sprang out of bed. I wanted to show Daddy the prints before he disappeared.

I heard him in the kitchen, but by the time I'd washed up and gone downstairs he was gone. I walked out onto the porch, smelling the strong sea air and the white beach plum blossoms that turned the trees into fluffy white clouds each June. I looked down the beach and saw Daddy leaping like a leprechaun over the rocks that he hated so much. He was heading east, toward the bridge and the puppet pond. He was moving very fast. I stumbled down the staircase and followed him, but when I reached the first bend in the shore I couldn't see him. I stood for a moment, listening, and thought I heard voices coming from the woods. But the breeze I'd awakened to had changed into a wind, and I turned back. I imagined Daddy roaming the woods, lost in the past that Lulu would not let him mourn.

23

I waited through the morning for Daddy to return. Around one o'clock, I joined Lulu in the garden. I sat cross-legged on the grass while she dug up weeds. One of Lulu's major triumphs was that she had managed to make grass grow in mostly sandy soil.

A rabbit rustled the shrubs behind her.

"Don't you come near here!" she shouted. The rabbit fled.

"Have you seen Daddy today at all?" I asked her.

"No," she said. "Not since we woke up."

"Where's he going?"

"I don't know."

"Doesn't he tell you?"

"I don't ask," she said.

"Doesn't it bother you that he's not working?" I asked.

"I'm sure he's thinking about it."

"Maybe he's thinking about you."

"I don't want to talk about that."

I ran my hands over the grass, fraying the line of her shadow.

Mosquitoes were buzzing around her legs, a few feet off the ground. She didn't seem to notice. Already her legs were the color of dark wood, and her back was so beautiful and brown that it was still hard for me to believe that something inside it was growing and making her weak.

24

By afternoon, I decided to go look for Daddy. I no longer wanted to show him my prints. I wanted to see if he was all right. I wanted to tell him I understood and that he could talk to me.

I followed the trail past the puppet stand and the pond out to the small bridge over the stream. I was halfway across it when I looked up and saw through the trees a large bright box, plunked down in the middle of the woods. It was raw plywood, unpainted, with a door but no windows. Daddy and Sam stood on ladders on either side of it, stretching a large piece of black canvas across the top to make a roof. They had built him a new studio.

I watched them from a distance, confused and annoyed. I had assumed that Daddy was thinking only of Lulu. In fact, it seemed as I watched him work and heard him laugh with Sam, he had created a perfect escape.

He saw me through the trees. I turned away. We were both angry.

"Jennifer!" he called from the ladder. "I want to talk to you."

"Later!" I shouted back childishly. "Lulu might need me."

25

"You were spying on me," Daddy said that night as we dug a pit on the beach to bake clams.

"I wanted to see if you were all right. I wanted to show you my new photographs."

"That doesn't make it right."

"I know."

"I was angry with you."

"I know. But Daddy. Lulu wants you to work. She told me. She doesn't want you to worry about her."

"I know," he said simply. "But I am working."

"You're just building a studio."

"But that's part of the work."

"How?" I asked.

"I don't want to tell you that now," he said.

I looked down at the hollow that we had dug and reached for some rocks that we had gathered for its sides.

"Are you just stalling for time?" I asked him.

"No," he said.

"Tell me then."

He repositioned the rocks I'd put in the pit, forming a star shape to replace my haphazard arrangement. It was a typical thing for him to do.

"Tell me," I said again. "Please."

"I can't, darling, not now."

"Do you need to get away from her?"

"No."

He smiled a private smile that I did not understand. He patted me vaguely on the shoulder and called to Hillary to bring down the clams. I thought he was running away from reality. It turned out that he would run least of all.

I never did show him my photographs, though. I gave the prints to Hillary and put my cameras away.

26

Spencer was arriving on Saturday, so Hillary spent all Friday getting ready. Not just Friday night. Friday. In the morning she ran four miles; she ran four in the afternoon, and in between she skipped rope on the deck while I lay in the sun, trying not to feel lazy.

"Daddy's building himself a new studio," I'd told her in a whisper a few nights before.

"Good for him," she'd said offhandedly, refusing to find it strange.

At five o'clock, Hillary washed her hair; at six her laundry. By six thirty she was standing in front of the mirror in our bathroom, putting her hair in curlers.

"I'm too pale," she said.

"I've never seen you more tan," I said.

At seven she was in the shower again, washing out the curls.

"*Marilyn,*" Lulu drawled when Hillary finally made her entrance on the stairs.

Spencer arrived the next day at noon. Tall, blond and, needless to say, handsome, he bounced into the house with a winning smile, and I had an instant crush on him. He looked like my runner friend Jim, but better. The grown-up version. He wore a beige V-neck sweater, no shirt, and a pair of madras Bermuda shorts. He was funny and quick, and clearly crazy about Hillary. She had told me he worked for an ad firm in Boston, and I could imagine him with clients. So what, I thought, if Lulu and Daddy had always called advertising the place for frustrated ambitions.

That may have been part of the reason for their coolness to him at dinner that first night, but I doubt it. It was probably just their customary distance from people outside the family. Poor Spencer. His face flushed as he tried small talk—politics, exhibits, plays. He was horribly uneasy, and I felt sorry for him. It was hard, stepping into this family. Lulu and Daddy were always pleasant and polite, but never exactly eager. They were already so content that they'd never felt the need to meet anyone, and that was easy to interpret as hostility. The best solution, of course, was to be as calm and casual as they were. But as I watched Spencer stammer his way along, I found myself wishing they could give a little more.

Late that night, Hillary and I happened to walk toward the bathroom upstairs at the same time.

"I can't believe the way they treated him," she whispered to me.

"I know."

"Can you imagine if we treated their friends that way?"

"They don't *have* any friends," I said sleepily.

She smiled wanly.

"They were rude," she hissed.

"They were Lulu and Daddy."

"Who the hell do they think they are?"

"Lulu and Daddy," I said.

27

I woke to the lonely sound of Spencer and Hillary making love. I felt jealous and crowded, and I took an early morning walk, wanting to get as far away from them as possible. I went down to the beach, stopping to pick up shells and look for sea glass, and I wandered to the old puppet stage.

The first time I had ever made love to anyone, it had been on the worn, warm floor of the puppet stage, out of sight of the house, with the sun on Richard's back and on my face. Afterwards, we had gone swimming, but we had put on our bathing suits. I had managed to get through the whole experience without once taking a real look at his body. When we made love, I had looked up at the rectangular frame of the puppet stage, and I'd seen the trees and the sky and an old osprey nest on a telephone pole. Later, I had returned to the spot. I had taken just that photograph, to remember the moment by.

28

A week had passed, another week of waiting for changes. Daddy mostly stayed out of sight. Lulu stayed in her garden, watching the beach plums and spireas and hydrangeas flower. Fallen petals streaked the lawn like puddles of white paint. Hillary laughed off my worries. She spent her time on the phone with Spencer or running the long dirt road till he returned.

On that Sunday, the twenty-fifth, Lulu was sitting in the kitchen on the fireplace bench, telling me how to cook the dinner.

"Nutmeg," she said, as I stood before the spice rack. "The secret to all great cooking is nutmeg."

"Nutmeg?"

"Yes."

"I'll have to remember that."

"You should. You've got to know these things."

I turned quickly to see what expression was on her face, but she had already looked away.

Hillary and Spencer came in, their hair dripping, their bare feet tracking sand.

"You'll have to sweep that up," I told Hillary after Spencer had gone upstairs to change. I could not help being jealous of her.

"I will," she said lightly. She bent down to kiss Lulu's forehead.

"How's my tan?" Hillary asked her.

"You look terrific."

"Isn't Spencer a dream?"

"He has a dreamy quality," Lulu said.

"I'm only having a salad tonight," Hillary continued, missing Lulu's irony and surveying my crowded stove. "Spencer bought a Beaujolais in town, by the way."

"Isn't that nice," Lulu said. "Now, get out of that wet bathing suit."

Hillary and I started to laugh.

"Quick," I said to Hillary. "Before you know what might happen."

"Did you know?" she said to me, reaching into the salad bowl for a cucumber. "Did you know, Jen, what happens to you if you don't get out of a wet bathing suit?"

"Of course," I said. "Medical fact."

"Rheumatism," we said to Lulu in unison. It was a famous Lulu maxim.

"I never told you that," she said.

"Oh, yes you did," we teased.

"And don't drink cold water after hot soup," Hillary said, "or your teeth will crack."

"I never said that either." But she was grinning now.

"And don't walk barefoot or you'll catch a cold," I said.

"Well, that's *true*," Lulu said, and Hillary and I kept laughing.

29

Hillary had insisted on candlelight for dinner. Daddy sat quietly, carving a small block of wood.

"Why don't you carve the chicken instead?" Lulu asked him.

"I don't work in chicken."

"I'll give you a hand," Spencer said.

The porch door was open so the flames jumped, and the hot wax quivered in the candlesticks, little pools. Lulu's face looked like wax, too, the part that wasn't in shadow. I got scared. I was scared even before she fell. It must have been how she looked in that light. You can't trust candlelight. You can barely shoot by it.

She stood up to get the salt, and she tripped.

"God!" Daddy shouted, letting his knife and his carving drop.

"Relax, relax," Lulu said quickly, but she was lying on her side on the floor and she was breathing fast. Her fists were clenched. "Nothing's happened," she said.

"You shouldn't have had any wine," Daddy said.

"I didn't."

"She didn't," I said. I had noticed.

Hillary crouched at Lulu's head, and Daddy was standing beside her. Spencer soaked a dish towel at the sink and brought it. I stood by the table and watched.

"That's very thoughtful, Spencer," she said.

I heard Daddy's voice shake. "Can you stand?" he asked.

"I'm not too crazy about the idea."

"Can you try?"

"No. Not yet."

"Not yet," I said.

I felt sick. I walked into their bedroom to straighten her pillows. I couldn't think what else to do. They carried her in, Spencer and Daddy, with Hillary holding her hand, and Daddy's face tightened, like a boy about to cry.

30

It took me a long time to fall asleep that night. I stayed up thinking. I knew that Lulu's fall had had nothing to do with her illness. I knew it had just been an accident. But it forced my thoughts forward and made me scared. I was letting time slip by. I was letting her convince me. If the accident was going to be in a plane, I thought, then I would have to learn about planes. I would have to take flying lessons.

I thought about just asking Lulu and Daddy to pay for them, but I figured that Daddy would jump at the excuse to leave the studio and would either want to teach me himself or to sit by watching my lessons. I couldn't have stood that. So I figured I'd tell Lulu that I wanted to learn and surprise Daddy. I knew she would like the normalness of that, the suggestion that our lives were going to be unchanged.

31

Lulu was still asleep in the morning when I left for the airport, so I wrote a note to her saying that I'd gone to take some photographs. I even brought my cameras with me. I drove with the radio on loud, and I stopped by the Episcopal church.

FOLLOW THE SONG OF YOUR HEART

it said in the window. Not bad, I thought.

At the airport, I found Harry back at his desk, his nondescript uniform looking freshly pressed, his bald head hidden by a matching cap.

"Who can teach me?" I asked him.

"Why not your dad?"

"He's too busy. He's working on something new," I said, wishing that it were true. "Anyway, I want to surprise him."

Harry told me I should learn with Benjamin Carr (he

pronounced it "Keah") and described the boy I'd seen the day I'd gone to pick up Hillary.

"But he's so young," I said.

"Best pilot I've got."

"You're sure."

"Trust your old friend, Jennifer. This guy should have his own pair of wings."

I thanked him and went out to the field. The air was hot and dusty, almost motionless. I smelled fuel, and burgers cooking from the airport diner. I scanned the rows of small planes and walked over the scorched grass. Benjamin Carr was at one of the last tie-downs, standing under the right wing of the yellow Cessna I'd seen last time. He still looked like a boy to me.

He was taking some fuel from the wing, though I didn't know then quite what he was doing. All I could tell was that he was holding what looked like a large syringe up to the sun. I walked up behind him.

"What are you looking for?" I asked.

He straightened up, startled, and bumped his head on the wing. Then he crouched down again.

"Bubbles," he said, annoyed, looking over his shoulder.

"Sorry about your head. Why bubbles?"

"Bubbles tell you if there's water in the gas tank."

"What happens if there's water in the gas tank?"

He sighed. "Champagne syndrome," he said gravely. "Plane gets drunk. Can't fly."

"I see."

He spilled the fuel out onto the grass and then turned to look at me, squinting, his head cocked to the left.

"You're Benjamin Carr?" I asked.

"That's me. You're the girl who was crying the other day."

I stared at him a second. "I was laughing before I was crying."

"I know. I noticed that too," he said. "It made me wonder." He wiped his hands on his blue jeans.

"How *old* are you?" I asked.

"Old enough."

"For what?"

"You tell me."

"Oh *please,*" I said. "What do you think? I want to learn to fly."

"Why?"

"What do you mean why? Why not?"

He shook his head, grinning. The grin helped his face. He had fine gray eyes and bushy eyebrows, straight brown hair and a preposterously large nose.

"Nope," he said. "That's just not good enough. Didn't anyone ever tell you not to answer a question with a question?"

"When did they tell you?"

He laughed. "That was another question."

"Was it?"

He only kept on grinning.

"Look," I said. "My father's been flying us to Sanders ever since I was a kid. He's always wanted me to learn how. Only I've been too scared. I thought it's be nice to surprise him."

"That's right, I know who you are," Benjamin said. "You're one of Milo Burke's girls." His eyebrows went up. "Are you the pretty one?"

"No," I said. "Didn't you see my sister land?"

"I was looking at you."

"How do you know who my father is?"

"A squirrel told me."

He led the way around the plane to the other wing.

"What's your name?" he asked as he readied the syringe.

"Jennifer," I said.

"Is it Jenny?"

"No. Never."

"Good."

"Is it Ben?"

He laughed, suddenly looking shy. He cocked his head again. "Well, just to old Harry in there," he said.

"Will you teach me to fly?"

"If you're going to surprise your old man, then how are you going to pay me?"

"My mom," I said. "How much will it cost?"

"Sixty dollars an hour."

"You're joking."

"Nope. That's the going price. Look," he said smugly, the shyness gone, "I know you can afford it. Be here at three sharp the day after tomorrow."

He was finished with the second wing and now stood looking down at me, his face in shadow.

"If you tell me why you were crying," he said, "I'll only charge you forty."

"Sixty dollars," I said, laughing. "I'll see you Wednesday."

32

Benjamin called his plane Oscar. That was short for the call letters, N5429O ("November-Five-Four-Two-Niner-Oscar"). He told me that pilots had started saying "niner" instead of "nine" during the war so people wouldn't think they were saying no in German. He told me about the phonetic alphabet—how each letter was represented by a word (*O* was Oscar and *N* was November). He spelled my name for me: Juliet Echo November November India Foxtrot Echo Romeo.

"Nice," he said. "Very romantic. I've got 'Alfa' and 'Mike' in mine."

"Sorry to hear it."

"Those are the breaks."

We met at the airport coffee shop before my first lesson. Benjamin told me that he had bought his plane for just $2,000 from an old pilot Harry knew on the Cape. It was a 1946 Cessna, and he had practically built a new engine for it. Benjamin had started flying when he was fourteen, and he had soloed the day of his sixteenth birthday. In the next few years he earned his private license, his commercial license, his instrument rating and his instructor's certificate. He'd been teaching in the summers for five years. Now he could fly a seaplane, a helicopter, a single engine and a twin. He was only twenty-three. He had sixteen hundred hours. Daddy, who had been flying for twenty years, had about a thousand.

Out on the grass, Benjamin started poking around the plane, a well-worn checklist in his hand.

"What are you doing?" I asked.

"Preflight."

"I *know* that. I mean what are you actually doing?"

"Little, confusing, mechanical things."

"Swell," I said.

"We'll get to them in time."

My heart was racing. "I want to know what I'm steering," I said. "I don't want to fly the way people drive. I want to know what makes it work. I'd rather not fly at all if I can't learn how the whole thing works."

"You will." He laughed. "Are you always this intense?"

I didn't answer. I just watched him finish the preflight. I tried to breathe slowly. I tried to calm down. It was only a flying lesson. I thought about all the times I'd watched Daddy do this same gentle dance around his plane. I didn't want to learn to fly. I hated flying. I hated the noise and the height and the turbulence, and most of all I hated having to rely on a series of springs and bolts.

It would be the end of the summer, I thought. We would transfer Lulu from a stretcher to the back seats of the plane. I would wave good-bye and watch them take off—

"Are you nervous?"

I was startled.

"Do I look nervous?"

"There you go again, answering questions with questions.'' He grinned. ''Nervous,'' he said, ''doesn't begin to describe the way you look. Get in.''

''Should I be flattered or insulted?'' I asked, climbing up on the wing.

''Depends.''

''On what?''

He leaned into my window conspiratorially.

''On what I meant when I said it.''

He shut my door. Once he'd climbed in on his side, he reached over to buckle my shoulder harness.

''This,'' he said, ''is how I get the girls.''

Swell, I thought. But then he looked at me quite seriously. ''There are no rules about the way you should be feeling,'' he said. ''If you're scared, or sick, or even ecstatic, it just doesn't count, okay? We're not going to be doing anything tough today. We're just going to go up and give you the feel of it. We'll be up about an hour. We're just going to try some straight-and-level flight, okay?''

''Okay,'' I said.

Benjamin shouted ''Clear'' out his window, then showed me how to steer on the hardtop with my feet. We taxied and waited for clearance.

''I think I'll take us up this time,'' he said.

''I like the way you think.''

We'd been up about five minutes when he turned to me with a winning grin.

''You do know how to land this thing, right?'' he asked.

''Nothing to it,'' I said.

JULY

1

I never knew if Lulu and Daddy collected famous people, or if famous people collected Lulu and Daddy. Probably it was a little bit of both, though Hillary and I grew up hearing that names should neither impress us ("I'm a name," Daddy would say, "and think what you know about me") nor be used to impress our friends. Namedropping was a sin tantamount to sloth and ignorance.

As children, Hillary and I were fairly good on the second point: we rarely let a name slip out, despite severe temptation. We failed miserably on the first point, though. We *were* impressed by names in those days, were secretly thrilled by the people who walked through our parents' living rooms in Boston and on Sanders, taking canapés from the trays we offered, asking us what grades we were in now and getting us mixed up with each other. We would giggle with glee when a well-known writer remembered who we were. We would rush off to the kitchen and report—verbatim—what some actor or artist or critic had said. And we were hopelessly disillusioned when a painter of otherwise mythic status had far too much to drink one night and stepped, fully clothed, into the ocean for a swim.

The people my parents knew were artists, of course, and their dealers and critics and backers. But with the "salon" types came journalists, novelists, poets, producers, directors and, much to Hillary's particular delight, an occasional film or Broadway star. Mostly my parents' acquaintances were people who shared the arrogance of creativity and of intellectual success. Their snobbism was based not on what they had inherited or assumed, but on what they had done or made.

In retrospect, I realize that was one of the reasons why Lulu enjoyed them, much as she complained about missing precious time alone with the three of us. In Lulu's Back Bay upbringing—and perhaps even more in her memory of it—people had always *had* more than they had *done,* and that had never impressed her. She believed that the people she and Daddy liked had earned their luxuries and their summer languor, had earned the right to celebrate themselves and one another. I think she almost enjoyed the scorn they had for society people. Society people bought their work, attended their openings, supported their galleries. But still they stood outside, and in many ways, Lulu's attitude toward them resembled her attitude toward Hillary and me. To *be* always seemed less important than to *do*.

Lulu had sent out the invitations for our annual July Fourth party a few weeks before she was diagnosed. I don't think she would have canceled it even if she had known about her illness first. Her sense of privacy, and of dignity, demanded that things seem "normal." She would not let her salon friends know, or The Boys, or Sam. Only the three of us and her doctors knew. I suspected that Hillary had told Spencer, but if she had, he didn't let on, and Hillary would never have admitted it to Lulu. Lulu did not want sympathy or probing questions or change. I've come to think now too that what she feared most in life was losing the control she had created. But I didn't see it that way then. I only saw her strength.

We hadn't tried very hard to argue with her about the party. By the first week of July, I had still seen only a few signs of her illness. There had been the bruises on her arms, which by now had faded. There were Daddy's growing absences, which somehow seemed more ominous. The reality of Lulu's illness, when it emerged, was as much of a shock to us as it was to her, and it took the form of a restless, impossible night—the night before the party. I took turns with Hillary and Daddy, stroking Lulu's back. Spencer was abandoned upstairs while the three of us sat up with Lulu, eyeing each other with fear.

That night, though it was only a hint of what was to come, I learned what real pain was because I watched Lulu learn. Real pain was the pain that persisted after she had taken painkillers and given them plenty of time to work and then taken more. Real pain left her feverish and ashen, with her knees hugged into her chest or her knuckles white around a pillow and her answers monosyllabic and a forced smile on her lips. Real pain seemed to me to be bigger and blacker than the ocean at night. It seemed a region that enveloped her, a place that was as sinister as it was private, and that we could not enter with her.

2

"What do you think now?" I asked Hillary the next morning as we combed our hair side by side in the bathroom mirror.

"Be quiet."

"Just keep pretending it isn't there."

"Be quiet."

"Just keep pretending."

But Lulu only glared at me when I asked her if she felt up to the party. And so she became Lulu again. She was full of instructions for Hillary and Daddy and me. Even Spencer was enlisted. Lulu wanted everything spotless—even more spotless than usual—and so we bought the groceries, cut fresh flowers, ironed the tablecloths, counted the chairs, put the extra leaves in the tables, cleaned the bathrooms, washed the windows, bought the liquor and made the ice cubes.

The four of us worked wordlessly through the afternoon, exhausted and edgy, choreographed by Lulu. I knew she was in pain, and I was furious at her for trying to pretend she wasn't. I didn't understand then that she needed to convince herself even more than she needed to convince everyone else.

A few times late in the day, Lulu disappeared into the bedroom, each time saying she had to check on something, each time staying away too long. Finally Daddy followed her in, and when he emerged fifteen minutes later, he had the same look on his face I'd seen the night she fell. I kept slicing vegetables until Spencer and Hillary went down to the beach for a break.

"Is she all right?" I asked him bitterly. "Are you?"

"No, she's not," he said, which startled me. I had never heard him admit something that she would have denied.

"Tell me," I said, feeling oddly detached. "Is it as bad as last night?"

"I don't think so," he said. "No."

"Couldn't we still call it off?"

"No."

"Bob Reese doesn't know?"

"No. And she doesn't want anyone to find out."

"Don't you want to tell Bob?"

"Of course I want to tell him. But we're not going to tell him."

"Oh, Daddy."

" 'No long faces,' she said." He looked at me squarely. "What we have to do," he said, "is use our imaginations. For as long as we possibly can."

Lulu was at the kitchen door before I could say anything to him.

"Did you get the candles?" she asked.

"Yes, Lulu," I said.

"Blue?"

"Blue."

"Good girl," she said.

Standing behind her, Daddy silently put a finger to his lips.

"Radishes in the salad for color?"

"Yes, Lulu."

"Cukes?"

"Yes."

"Peeled? Sliced thin?"

"Yes."

"What's wrong with you?" she asked.

"Nothing."

"In two hours, there will be twenty-six people in this house. Where's Hillary?"

I laughed. "On the beach. With Spencer."

"Fabulous," she said.

3

By six o'clock, I had put the salad in the fridge, laid out the cheese boards and the crackers, set the table and put the VW in the garage. I went outside to take a shower. That was another of Lulu's creations: she had asked Sam to build a kind of booth in the woods. It had a high Dutch door that Sam had sawed open on a slightly crooked line. You could look at the trees and the sky and still have your privacy. It was a wonderful shower. Spiders tended to live in the corners, but Daddy always killed them for me. It was especially good for singing, because no one could hear you.

That evening I sang Lulu's song, turning the water up as hot as I could stand it, trying to banish the sleepless, numb feeling and the images of Lulu from the night before.

Them that's got shall get
Them that's not shall lose
So the Bible says
And it still is news:

Mama may have, and Papa may have
But God bless the child
That's got his own . . .

I closed my eyes and sang louder, and then Hillary was pounding on the shower door.

"You'll use up all the hot water," she said.

I opened my eyes to see her peering over the Dutch door.

"Hello," I said.

"Come on."

Then she disappeared. She left the breeze through the trees again and one black bird that lit on a branch and flew off.

But God bless the child
That's got his own . . .

I turned the water off and stepped out onto the deck, darkening the wood with my wet feet. From the clothesline, I pulled down a towel still warm from the sun. Lulu had left it for me. I wrapped it around me and went upstairs to change.

4

I was still trying to figure out what to wear when the first car pulled up. I looked out my window and saw Spencer awkwardly extending his hand to Kevin Gross, a critic, and his wife, Betina.

It was still light enough to see the rabbits scampering on the lawn.

I dressed quickly and went downstairs. Daddy was slicing lemons at the bar. He looked at me grimly but said nothing. In the bedroom I found Lulu and Hillary standing before the full-length mirror. They were both in black—Hillary in black pants and a black silk scarf that she had tied as a halter, her back and shoulders as brown as Lulu's. Lulu was wearing a floor-length caftan with a high collar.

They turned to look at me as I came in: twin blond statues, their beauty and their resemblance to one another a reproach. I had always felt like a lesser version of them. My white silk shirt and white jeans seemed shabby.

The house filled up quickly. As always, the guests fell

into four categories that Hillary and I had identified years before: there were the familiar and friendlies, the familiar and unfriendlies, the unknowns and the unknowables.

I hid in the kitchen as long as I could, needlessly slicing carrots. Then Daddy sauntered into the dining room with Bob. Behind them was the dread Althea, draped in something pink.

"Here she is," Bob said, a familiar and friendly.

"Jennifer," Daddy said. "Come say hello to Bob and Althea."

I kissed Bob on the cheek, and Althea extended a droopy hand. The familiar and unfriendly category had been created for Althea.

In the living room, guests stood in twos and threes, the women in caftans and shawls, the men in blue blazers and Lacostes or turtlenecks. The summer residents were tan, the weekenders were sunburned, and the islanders were pale. Spencer and Hillary were talking intensely to one another on the couch, as if they had just been introduced. I decided I didn't like Spencer. Spencer was a ship in a bottle. He had gotten into our family somehow, and it seemed that he wasn't going to come out until the bottle broke.

I picked up the cheese tray and began to make the rounds. By the north window stood two unknowables: Humphrey and Delilah Elliott. Humphrey Elliott was a novelist. He had written a book a year for twenty-four years. The latest one had just been made into a movie (its director, Walton Lindsay, had also come and was standing by the bar—one for Hillary, I thought).

Elliott (he never allowed himself to be called Humphrey) was a drunk, and a very pompous drunk. Daddy had run into him at the drugstore the week before. Elliott had asked him whether Walter Valance, the publisher, was invited to our party. Daddy had said he was. And Elliott had answered, without a trace of a smile: "I'm not sure I'll be able to stomach that, Milo."

But if Elliott was bad, his wife was even worse. Delilah came from the South and had a talent for making people feel sorry they hadn't come from the South, too. Oozing was her forte. "Sincerity," Daddy once said about her, "is not Delilah's strong suit."

"Well, don't you look cunning," she gushed at me as I offered her the cheese tray. "No. Not for me, dear. You know how it puts on pounds."

"Oh, but Mrs. Elliott," I said, trying to say just what Lulu would, "you can't be worried about your weight."

"Aren't you sweet to say so. Dear?" And she turned to Elliott, who was grimly twirling the ice cubes in his glass. "Isn't Hillary lovely tonight?"

"I'm Jennifer," I said.

5

By eight o'clock, Ilka (familiar and friendly) was standing by Daddy's beach drawings, surrounded by an audience. Ilka had no last name. She was just Ilka. She was probably already eighty that summer, and she looked that old but didn't move that way. When you were with Ilka, you always felt you'd been wasting time. She reminded me of Lulu.

Ilka was a sculptor, and a superb one. She had managed to get out of Hungary before the Communists came in. In America, she simply continued the work she'd been doing in Budapest as if she had never left it, or her family, or anything else, behind. Ilka used found objects in her sculptures—dominoes, dolls' heads, playing cards, door-knobs. She said, too, that she couldn't draw. She said her art was assemblage, not creation, and that reminded me of photography. I was not the only one who thought she was brilliant and original, and I also loved her. She was like the good queen in fairy tales. I could always imagine her in ermine and emeralds, though in fact she dressed very simply.

"*Ma petite,*" she said from across the room, with a vaguely regal gesture.

"Can I get you anything?" I asked her after she had kissed me on both cheeks.

"No, no," she said in her wonderful rolling accent. "But you must tell me things." She leaned toward me intently, excluding all the others. Ilka always smelled of strong soap and perfume. When we were close together, that smell made me feel strange and melancholy. I think it was Ilka who first made me realize that my parents would grow old. She had frightened me once, as old people usually frighten children.

She took me by the hand, her heavy gold chain bracelets clinking against one another. She led me out to the porch. From the corner of my eye, I could see Lulu introducing Hillary to Walton Lindsay, and Spencer standing by like an eager, sunburned footman.

"I need to know several things," Ilka said, still holding my hand as we walked toward the salt breeze coming up from the ocean. "First of all," she said, "what little magics have you been putting on film?"

"Oh, Ilka."

"Come, come. Is the book out yet?"

"Yes," I said. "It just came."

"Then I must see it."

"I'd like that."

"And now? Has the new work been good?"

"I thought so," I told her. "But Daddy didn't like it."

"You did?"

"Until he saw it, yes."

"You must trust your own instincts," she said.

I laughed. "I know. He told me the same thing. But I don't know how to ignore him. Everything he says sounds true."

She laughed, dismissing what I'd said as a joke. I kissed her on the cheek.

She turned away from me to face the dark ocean. As I turned, I looked in the window and saw Hillary hugging Frederick Perry, a writer I had a crush on. Walton Lindsay was looking on, obviously charmed.

Ilka was still holding my hand. Before us, only the shore was lighted by soft squares from the window. There was no moon.

"What else do you need to know?" I asked.

Her bracelets clinked again as she let go of my hand to tuck a strand of white hair behind her ear.

"Your mother," she said. "She does not look well. And I'm not being a catty female. You are going to tell me what it is."

"What it is," I repeated, surprised that she had noticed the physical change in Lulu.

"Yes. You are going to tell me."

For a moment, seeing our shadows on the sand below the deck, I thought I might. I imagined how awful she would feel when she learned that Lulu had died without a word of good-bye.

"No," I said brightly. "I don't think it's anything. I know what you mean, but I think she's just tired."

Ilka sighed, then briskly turned back to face the house.

"Well, of course I don't believe you," she said. "You are not telling me the truth, and this does disappoint me."

She left me standing by the railing with the sound of the waves, and my vague shadow on the sand below. It would be the end of the summer. Lulu would be lifted into the back seats of the plane. We would have to remember to bring pillows. . . . But it was cold on the porch, with the wind picking up.

6

Back inside, it seemed the cocktail noises had deepened. The guests were already making their slow but inevitable slide from apprehension to expansiveness. I knew the giddiness would come later.

I stood for a few moments near the living room door, feeling like a little girl on her first day of school. Hillary had disappeared. My writer Frederick was now deep in conversation with Ilka. He winked at me as I passed by. He had probably forgotten my name. His wife, whom I hated reflexively, was standing at his side, following the conversation as if it were a tennis match, laughing when they laughed. I saw Walton Lindsay talking to one of the unknowns, and I looked for Lulu. Then I heard her laugh. She was sitting on the couch between Althea Reese and an alarmingly pink-cheeked Humphrey Elliott. Lulu looked over at me and raised her left eyebrow at Elliott. He followed her glance, but not her meaning.

"Ah, Hillary," Elliott said.

"This is Jennifer, Elliott," Lulu said.

"Jennifer," he repeated thickly. "Be an angel and fill my glass."

Lulu shot me a warning look.

"Scotch?" I asked him sweetly, taking his glass.

"Good girl! You've trained them well, Katherine."

I headed for the bar in the foyer. Daddy was standing there, listening to Butler Evans. You didn't have much choice with Butler Evans. He was not very good at traditional conversational skills. It was either silence or monologue. He was a very brilliant architect, but he spoke at subnormal speed, and people always assumed that he was stoned. He wasn't. If you listened carefully, you found yourself caught up in the rhythm of his thoughts, and you learned after a while that his pauses were significant and appropriate—and never left dangling. But listening was still a challenge.

"So there was this captain," Butler was saying as I watered down Elliott's Scotch. Butler's fine blue eyes were glassy, his voice as low and blurry as his eyes. "This sea captain." He looked up at me, neither including me nor excluding me from the monologue. "This sea captain had built an old house. Long ago." (With this, he patted the foyer wall.) "It was crumbling, this old house, and covered with vines. The vines were all that was holding up the house. Vines. But then he went away on a long sea voyage and found treasures. Treasures. And when he came back, he came back . . . he had found treasures, see, so he added on dormer windows to his house, and then a porch overlooking the sea . . ."

"Excuse me, Butler," Daddy said.

He walked over to me, leaving Butler in mid-thought.

"What was he telling you about?" I whispered. "What sea captain?"

Daddy smiled. "I think that was his way of saying it's time for us to renovate."

We giggled softly together.

"Are we almost ready to eat?" he asked.

"I think so. Humphrey Elliott's getting broiled."

"That's what makes him Humphrey Elliott. Where's Lulu?"

"With him," I said. "On the couch. Trapped between Elliott and Althea."

"Brave woman, your mother."

"Ilka asked me what was wrong with her."

"What'd you say?"

"I said nothing."

"What'd she say?"

"She didn't believe me. Daddy, how long do we have to lie?"

"I don't know." He pushed his glasses up on his nose. "I know. You hate it when I say that," he said. "But you're going to have to get used to it." He turned to go back to Butler.

I decided to abandon Elliott's glass, and I walked toward the kitchen, squeezing past a few unknowns, smiling at their feet.

On the stove, steam was rising from six huge pots—four filled with lobster and two with corn. A pan of butter sat among them. I could smell caraway seeds and the melting butter. Hillary and Spencer—like the inevitable statue—were kissing on the fireplace hearth, again apparently oblivious to their surroundings.

"How's it coming?" I asked.

Hillary disengaged herself before Spencer did, pressing a demure hand against his knee. Frederick, I thought. Jim. Richard on the puppet stand. I thought about the two brief, embarrassing flings I'd had that year at school.

"The lobsters," Hillary announced, "are dead."

"How could you do it, Hills?"

"I don't know. Something just came over me."

Spencer giggled.

"Daddy's upset about Lulu," I said, ignoring him completely.

"He seems fine to me," she said. She stood up and turned off the flames under the lobsters. "Remember what we talked about?" she asked. "About crisis time?"

"Yes."

"Well, this isn't it."

"But last night—"

"She just had a bad night."

"Ilka asked me what was wrong with her."

"What'd you say?"

"I said nothing."

"Good."

"How was Walton Lindsay?" I asked.

"Great. He told Lulu I was delightful."

"And you are," Spencer chimed in.

"How true," I said.

"Do the salad."

As I reached into the refrigerator, I heard the click of Lulu's sandals on the dining room floor.

"Girls," she said, "how's it coming?"

"We're ready as soon as everyone sits down," Hillary said.

"How do you feel?" I asked.

"Fine. Stop asking. Why aren't there salad bowls on the table?"

"I thought we'd use the plates," I said.

"That's silly. There won't be room."

"Sure there will."

"Don't argue with me. Put the bowls on the table and then tell everyone to sit down."

7

In the living room, I tried to get everyone's attention, but Humphrey Elliott outdid me.

"I don't care what the lousy critics say," he was shouting at Walter Valance, the publisher. "Why the hell do I *need* to care?"

Delilah was squeezing her husband's arm in support. Ilka was whispering something to Frederick. Daddy and Butler were just walking in from the foyer.

"Take Milo here," Elliott continued. "He's never listened to the critics. They've been saying he's washed up for *years*."

"Elliott—" Daddy began.

"Oh, come on now, Milo. You don't have to be a critic like Mr. Gross over here to know what the real story is with you. Do you, Kevin? One subject. One subject! And why are you standing way over there anyway, Kevin?"

Walter Valance took a step forward.

"It's refreshing," he said drily, "to see that some things never change. You're still an irredeemable bore, Elliott."

"Tell me," Elliott said, a frightening smile on his face.

Daddy tried again. "Elliott. Walter."

Hillary walked in. I met her eyes. She looked back at me, bewildered. Everyone else was staring at the floor. The conversation and the drinking had stopped.

"Spectacular," Elliott said. "Valance, you're spectacular."

"Boys."

Lulu was standing in the doorway. They looked up, just as if they had been caught playing hooky or smoking after school. "You're upsetting me." There was a long, noble pause, and Lulu smiled her most haughty smile. "You're being a drip, Elliott," she said. Walter started to straighten up. "And you, Walter, you're just encouraging him. Now cut it out. You know you both respect each other or you wouldn't bother to argue. Six lobster pots are steaming up my kitchen windows, and it's time for dinner."

8

As usual, Lulu had pondered the seating arrangements very carefully. She had made only one last-minute change: separating Walter and Elliott. The guests were divided between two tables in the living room and one in the dining room. I sat between Daddy and Frederick in the dining room, but Frederick spent most of the time talking to Ilka, who was seated on his right.

There was a lot of wine, and the laughter slipped up a notch. I felt giddy and disconnected. I could hear Elliott from the next room, his voice rising over the others and at one point a fist, which I knew was his, pounding the table.

"Damn," Daddy said quietly.

I met up with Hillary in the kitchen when I went to get the coffee.

"How's Lulu doing?" I asked her.

"Lulu's doing fine," Lulu said, appearing suddenly. "Hills, let us alone a minute."

I fussed with the coffeepot, waiting.

"Now look, Jennifer," she began. "I've really had enough of this. I've got enough on my mind with Walter and Elliott and that awful Althea Reese. I want you to stop right now."

"But Lulu."

"But Lulu *what*? Wipe that look off your face. I won't have it."

I stared at the kitchen floor, tracing the flowers and birds in the tiles. Once a bird had flown into the living room window, thinking the window was the sky. It had landed on the deck, screaming and fluttering and trying to fly. Lulu had had Sam shoot it.

"Don't you think it's tough enough for me?" she asked.

"That's just the point," I said passionately. "Don't you see, Mom?" I asked. "We don't want you to have to go through this."

"Well, that's just too bad. I don't want these people to know. I thought Daddy explained that to you."

"But they're friends."

"I know."

"They're going to be hurt."

"My health," she said furiously, "is none of their business."

"How can you say that?"

"It's *my* business."

"How do you think they'll feel when they find out?"

"They're not *going* to find out," she said.

In the endless moment that followed, I realized what was happening. I was telling her that she was going to die. She was telling me that she wasn't going to die. But I could not stop myself. I think I needed to feel important—the meddler, the bearer of secrets. I think I simply needed her to stop being so strong. There can be a kind of prison in a parent's strength.

"Daddy," I said, "thinks they will. Daddy says he's tired of pretending."

She stepped back as if I had pushed her, but she didn't

look hurt. She looked hateful. She stared at me the way she would have stared at a drunken stranger. She took a step forward and slapped my face and then walked, head high, from the room.

I ran out the door and down to the beach, crying. I fell over an old piece of driftwood and cut my knee. I still have the scar. I cried very hard. I mouthed the word Lulu and that made me cry harder. My mother was dying. Her body was dissolving away from her. Her skin was changing color and her hair was getting thin and she would not change. She would not lie down. She would not act like a dying woman, would not grant us the haven of feeling sympathy and outrage and pity and sorrow. But I had made her hate me, and I was crying beyond reason, hugging myself on the windy beach, watching the bright windows of the house as they blurred into disembodied rectangles. She hated me and I was a small child, empty and terrified.

An hour must have passed. My throat ached from crying, and my nose was stuffed. Then I heard her call my name and saw her standing halfway down the stairs to the beach. I shouted back and ran to her, again stumbling over the rocks. I didn't have to know then how to comfort myself. What I knew and needed was in her arms.

"I'm sorry, Jennifer," she said. "My little girl."

I couldn't speak. We stood, embracing, with the wind whipping our hair against each other's faces, and the waves coming in like whispers.

9

I resolved to change. I resolved that I would never again let her see me weak. She was strong and I would be just as strong. I would act the way she wanted me to.

The next morning, Lulu asked Hillary to take her into town to shop, and I went to find Daddy in his studio. If I couldn't take care of her, I thought, then I would take care of him.

Once at the studio, though, I stood for a long time outside the door, waiting. If Lulu had told Daddy about our scene the night before, then he would be furious at me for telling her what he'd said. But I guessed—correctly, it turned out—that she would have avoided that confrontation too.

There were still no windows in the studio, so I couldn't look in. I could hear Daddy, though. I could tell that he was planing wood. I heard him humming in time to his work. I couldn't make out the song. But I imagined him inside, and mixed with the delight I felt at the thought of him finally working was the horrible image of him working without

Lulu. She had been his only model. She had been every nude he ever made. From now on, I realized, he would have only other sculptures of her to carve from. A lot of stone and wood, and no flesh. It would be the end of the summer, and I would rescue my father from the stone and the wood and the no flesh. I opened the studio door.

"Jennifer!"

"I'm sorry!"

We spoke simultaneously, our first words like a crossing of swords. Only I did not want to fight with him. I wanted to console and comfort him, to be his confidante.

"I told you I'd show you when *I* was ready."

"Oh, Daddy," I said.

I hadn't moved. Daddy had not been carving a nude at all. He had been carving a wooden horse. It was a huge and powerful and funny horse, and another, much like it, stood behind him. That one was finished, and it was already the motley, gay colors of our marionettes. Colors. He hadn't used colors since the day he had carved our last puppet. A gesture to Lulu, I thought, a last acknowledgment of her insight.

I walked slowly toward the finished horse. Its head was turned jauntily to one side, which made me think of Benjamin. Its hooves were lifted in mid-prance. Its saddle was fluted like corduroy, finely striped, and the pommel was a rose. Its neck, like the necks of Daddy's nudes, was stretched out elegantly. It was fantastic and beautiful, but all I saw in it then was a gesture to Lulu: truce, surrender, spoils.

"Daddy," I said, overwhelmed with pity.

He said nothing, just kept planing the back of the new horse—working and working the already smooth surface, the plane like a third hand.

"Don't be angry," I said. "I just came to see if you were all right."

"I'm all right, darling," he said. "Are you?"

"She made it hard last night."

"I know. Hand me that," he said, pointing to a pocketknife on a sawhorse by the far wall. I stepped through a maze of paint cans, tools and sketches.

"No one wants to talk about it," I said.

"You can talk to me any time you want."

I handed him the pocketknife. "Horses," I said gently. "You've never done horses before."

He nodded.

"Like *Neptune's Horses*?" I asked, wanting to show him I remembered.

He looked up and smiled.

"In a way," he said.

"You're doing this for Lulu," I said softly. "Because of the puppets. The colors," I said. I stroked the nose of the finished horse as if it were alive.

He didn't answer me.

"Daddy?"

"I don't want you to tell Lulu or Hills."

"Why not?"

"Because I said so."

"All right."

"Not until I'm ready."

"All right," I said sadly. "How many are you going to do?"

He looked up, grinning, and opened his small arms as wide as they could go. "A carousel," he said. "It's going to be a ten-horse, wooden, Burke carousel."

"You're going to build the whole thing in here?" I asked.

He nodded. "Sam's going to help with the centerpiece."

"That's why you needed a bigger studio?"

"Right."

"When will you show Lulu?"

"I don't know. When it's done, I suppose."

"Have you told her about the studio?"

"Yes."

"But she doesn't know what you're doing?"

"No."

I watched as he returned to his planing, back and forth, his head down, his whole body tense, as if he couldn't stop.

10

When I got back to the house, Hillary and Lulu had returned from town. Something must have happened while they were there, something even more forceful than the night before the party. Or maybe it was just that with Spencer back in Boston, that night had finally caught up with Hillary. In any case, after Lulu had gone to her bedroom to lie down, Hillary didn't rush off to call Spencer, or go for a run, or practice her balcony scene. She began to unpack the groceries. She didn't tell me to do it, didn't even ask me to help, and when I pitched in, she thanked me.

"You all right?" I asked as I watched her fold up the empty brown bags.

"Fine."

"Talk to Spencer?"

"He just left."

"That's never stopped you before."

She shrugged. She turned to put the bags away.

"Is Lulu all right?" I asked.

"She's tired."

"Remember," I said, wanting to be nice, "that it's not crisis time yet."

"Why don't you just stop talking," she said.

"Want me to test you on your lines?"

"Leave me alone," she said. She walked out onto the porch and let the door close loudly behind her.

11

I left for my second flying lesson at around two thirty. I thought of Daddy working over his carving, smoothing it over, leaning into it as if it was their life.

My first lesson had been fair. After all, not much had been expected of me. I had held the yoke, gingerly moving the elevator and the ailerons. I had tried "straight-and-level" and told Benjamin it felt more like curved and bumpy. When I'd hit a bad patch of air pockets, I had panicked and asked him to take over, and he had.

This time, Benjamin took me through an abbreviated preflight, showing me the basic parts of the plane: the empennage, the fuselage, the ailerons, the rudder, the engine.

"How does it all work?" I asked.

He grinned. "We'll get to that." He folded his yellow rag neatly in quarters and said, "Come on, I want to show you something before we start."

Benjamin taxied and took off, and we climbed above the

clouds. They were white mountains with small peaks of blue. They were a sea of Neptune's horses.

"What do you think?" he asked through the headset.

I could not stop smiling, and Benjamin said later it was that smile that won him over. It certainly wasn't my flying. The lesson itself was worse than the one the week before. Back under the clouds, Benjamin said, "Get the feel of it!" I held my yoke while he moved his violently to the left and right and in and out. "See?" he shouted as the plane slipped wildly back and forth. "Pretty tight!" he said. "Not like power steering!" But every time I started to think I had it, I'd feel the nose dipping down. I'd try to correct it by pulling back on the yoke, then find my view half obscured by the nose rising. I felt shaky and scared.

The clouds thinned, and the three o'clock light was blinding. I realized I'd forgotten my sunglasses. The cabin was hot because Benjamin's air vent was stuck, and I noticed that there were crumbs all over the seat and on the floor.

We circled the island six times, Benjamin happily pointing out landmarks that he said I should aim for. The panel of instruments blurred into meaningless white markings on black, an endless configuration of dominoes.

He asked me to execute turns I could not do, to handle climbs and descents that I missed by huge degrees. I was frustrated, embarrassed and often just scared. By the time we landed and tied Oscar down, I could barely manage a smile.

"I guess I'm a slow learner," I said, not wanting to look at him as we walked across the grass.

Benjamin didn't answer, just shuffled along beside me.

"You'll see," I continued. "I'll get the hang of it."

"Well, sure," he said, and his grin was suddenly infuriating. I caught his eye and glared a good Hillary glare. He laughed. "Really," he said. "I'm sure you will."

Jerk, I thought.

"How about a post-second-lesson cup of coffee?" he asked.

"No thanks."

"It's a flying tradition," he said.

"No."

"Don't be sore."

"I'm *not* sore," I said, turning to leave. "I'll see you next Wednesday."

12

At night I dreamed of flying, unencumbered, over the banks of the clouds. I was not in a plane and I did not have wings. I merely moved, face into the wind, my chin raised like Lulu's, my whole body pointing toward another shore, free. I woke conscious of three separate lights: the sun rising beyond the window, the stereo amplifier I had left on across the room and the driveway light that no one had remembered to turn out. The amplifier buzzed and hummed. I heard Hillary in the kitchen below.

When I fell back to sleep, I was flying again, only this time inside Benjamin's plane, which was suddenly crowded with instruments—not just on the front panel but on the doors and the ceiling and the floors as well. I looked at Benjamin in panic, and he grinned silently.

13

Two days later, the four of us sat around the kitchen hearth drinking hot chocolate. It was raining, and Lulu was feeling good. She sat with her long legs elegantly crossed, composing a want ad for the *Sanders Island Sentinel*.

"Wanted," she read aloud as Hillary stirred a batter for pancakes. "Wild white daisies."

"You can't *advertise* for *daisies*," I said.

"Yes you can," Hillary said protectively.

Lulu raised her eyebrow and lifted her chin.

"You never know," she said.

Daddy and I exchanged a glance.

Lulu told us that she wanted to go to the Cape on her annual antiques hunt. We tried to talk her out of it, but it was no use. Reluctantly, I agreed to be her traveling sidekick and chauffeur. Hillary said she wanted to clean out the garage. She said she wanted to memorize her lines. Daddy said he would fly Lulu and me over to the mainland, drop us off and pick us up at the end of the day.

"You be the grown-up," he told me.

When he and Hillary left the kitchen, I told Lulu that I wanted to surprise Daddy by taking flying lessons. I told her Harry had said he'd found someone to teach me. I asked her if she would pay for the lessons. I did not tell her that I'd been up already. But as I'd expected, she was completely delighted by the idea. I was telling her the opposite of what I'd told her the night of the party. I was telling her that I could spare some of my time with her.

14

It was only eight o'clock when the three of us left for the airport Saturday morning, and we were halfway there before I remembered that I hadn't called Benjamin to warn him. I wondered if he would have the good sense not to say anything that would give me away.

We drove through the quiet morning. We passed a white-haired woman in a sky blue windbreaker who was fishing from the Sanders bridge. Several kids my age were already out on the roads, thumbing for rides. Daddy was grim and silent as he drove. Lulu looked around with exaggerated enthusiasm. I sat in the back seat, wondering if I could talk to Benjamin before he said anything.

At the airport, Daddy dropped Lulu and me at the gate, then went to park the car. Lulu had complained the day before that one of the drugs she was taking left a bad taste in her mouth, and she wanted to find some mints. We went into the terminal. Together we walked down the dingy corridor to the candy and cigarette machines.

"Well, hello there."

Benjamin was standing next to Harry in the radio room.

"Hi," I said, and kept walking.

As Lulu and I waited on the blue bench for Daddy to return, she asked:

"Who was that boy?"

"He's Harry's pilot."

"He looks so young."

"That's what I said. But Harry says he's the best around."

Lulu raised her eyebrow.

"Have you been up with him?"

"No, not yet," I said. "But I'm going up on Wednesday."

In the cool air, with only the distant sound of cars arriving and the faint sputter of static on the loudspeaker, Lulu looked at me more closely.

"How was it?" she asked, flawlessly Lulu—insightful, angry and forgiving all at once.

I laughed. "I'm not very good," I said.

"Well, be careful."

I gave her a hug, careful now not to hug too hard. Daddy came back looking worried.

"Are you sure you want to do this, kid?" he asked.

She tossed her shoulders back and looked beautiful. She gazed at him; he didn't say anything else. We walked out to the plane, and I watched more carefully this time as Daddy did his preflight. Prop, gas tank, ailerons, rudders—where was the weakness? It would be the end of the summer. As we took off, I could see Benjamin standing alone on the runway by his yellow plane with his yellow rag in his hand. I watched until he became just two yellow dots on a background of green and gray.

15

Lulu and I rented a car at the Barnstable airport and said good-bye to Daddy, who had continued to look glum and doubtful.

"I'll be back at six," he told me as Lulu fished in her handbag for the instructions that The Boys had given her over the phone. "Don't let her overdo it," he whispered to me.

"How do I manage that?"

Lulu and I drove for miles past wooden windmill signs and roadside astrologers, past backyards filled with pottery and dust, past all the fast-food places and the gas stations. She chattered away happily, talking about what we might find, recalling past coups from past summers. "Remember that grandfather clock Hillary and I found in Fall River? Remember the checkerboards?" And there we were again—a day just like any I had ever spent with her. Maybe she won't let herself, Hillary had said.

"Here!" Lulu cried, pointing toward a street sign.

I turned off the main road while Lulu peered at the notes she had made, trying to read her own handwriting.

"Left," she said.

We found a narrow country lane. Lulu rolled down her window, and we could smell the hyacinths and beach roses that lined the road.

"Here!" she said again.

I pulled over in front of an old gray Cape Cod house with an antiques sign painted in tiny black letters on a weathered split-rail fence. Anyone but Lulu would have missed it. I parked the car and climbed out. It took Lulu a bit longer, but there was a gleam in her eye.

"Come on, Jen," she said, leading the way.

A bell jangled softly as Lulu opened the faded green door. A sleeping golden retriever lifted his head slightly, then put it down again. The room was large and stuffy. It was dark except where the sunlight came in through the small windows, lighting the dust. No one was around.

"You take the high road and I'll take the low road," Lulu said.

For ten or fifteen minutes, we snaked our way silently through row after row of junk. It wasn't even good junk, the kind with hidden treasures. This was real junk: tarnished frying pans, plastic plates, stained dolls, bad paintings. The furniture was just as bad as the bric-a-brac: painted wood dressers and flimsy bookshelves, some covered with faded wallpaper. Dutifully, I kept looking. You never knew. I had been with Lulu on too many expeditions when she had followed my footsteps and then said, "How could you have missed this?" But there was nothing, absolutely nothing. I started to giggle. Lulu looked up from across the room, laughing and holding out a rusted barbecue grill.

"How much am I bid for this?" she asked.

"You tell me," I said.

"Let's get out of here," Lulu said. "It's awful."

"Where do you think the owners were?" I asked as I followed her through the front door.

"That dog *was* the owner."

"So that was The Boys' great suggestion?"

"Maybe it's farther down the road."

I started for the car, but Lulu was already walking ahead.

"Don't you want to drive?" I asked.

"No," she said. "It's lovely."

I thought about trying to make her ride. Don't let her overdo it. But I was powerless, and I knew it. I had already let myself believe exactly what she wanted me to believe.

The road twisted and widened. We kept walking. There were virtually no cars. We passed cows staring sleepily from behind barbed wire, and one red farmhouse after another.

"We're going to get lost," I said. "Let's go back."

"Maybe just around the bend," she said. How typical, I thought. Just around the bend. You never know. It'll all blow over.

After about ten minutes we saw another gray house, this one huge, flat and rambling. GENERAL STORE, the sign said, and underneath it ANTIQUES, and a scroll: FURNITURE, PAINTINGS, SUNDRIES. OPEN SUNDAYS. Lulu led the way. The front porch was sagging and loaded down with objects: an old upright vacuum cleaner with a punctured bag; several plastic buckets; a washing machine covered with padding; a scale that said CHARACTER READINGS! YOUR FUTURE!, and above it a frying pan, a FOR SALE sign and a COME ON IN WE'RE OPEN sign.

"Oh, Lulu," I said. "Another one."

"Let's see."

The ceiling was low, the front room small and crowded and no brighter than the first place. Three electric fans circulated the stale air. We could hear a woman talking in another room. We started our hunting again: old records, old *Life* and *National Geographic* magazines. Off the main room were five or six others, each overflowing with dubious relics. One room was filled with glass cabinets, and I paused before what looked like good Wedgwood china.

"Lulu," I called. She came up behind me. I pointed to the plates and cups.

"Fake," she said instantly. "Really, Jen."

"Sorry."

I walked across the hallway to another room and perched on an old school desk that was covered with ink stains and carved initials. I lit a cigarette. I heard the fans moving back and forth and heard Lulu's footsteps as she prowled the rooms intently. Daddy had told me once that when he met her, Lulu was on an archaeology kick and had read all the books she could find on the subject. Watching her sift through the piles of broken, discarded things, I could easily imagine her in the sands of some distant desert, digging with her bare hands if necessary.

"Don't you want to look?" she called.

"You look."

"You're not tired already, are you?"

"No, I'm not tired already," I said.

I was tired, though, and claustrophobic, and I was hungry, too.

"Oh, Jen!" she called.

"What?"

"My *God*."

"Lulu?" I hopped off the desk.

"Come look. Oh, *Jen!*"

I followed her voice down the hall. I found her in a closet of a room. She was standing, triumphant, with a dark wooden object in her arms. An expression of pure delight crossed her face. Her eyes were shining like Daddy's, and her shoulders were square.

"What is it?" I asked gently.

"Look!" she said, holding the object farther out for my inspection. I looked, then started laughing. It was a wooden rabbit—that much I could tell—with four wildly misshapen paws. Its ears were slicked back ridiculously, lying flat against its back. In its mouth was what looked like a large flat spoon with teeth. The spoon part was rusted the same dark color as the wood.

"What is it?" I asked again, starting to giggle.

"Don't you know?" She sounded genuinely surprised.

"Well, I figure it's a rabbit," I said. "Beyond that, I wouldn't want to guess."

"Don't be silly," she said, with her eyebrow arched. "I know exactly what this is."

"You do."

"I do. It's a trowel."

"A trowel?"

"Yes. It's a trowel. It's extremely old. People used this to dig."

"To dig what?"

"To dig. You know. For planting. In Africa."

"In Africa," I said, still giggling.

"Now stop that. Don't be a smart aleck." She looked around excitedly. "Where's that woman? Didn't you hear a woman when we came in? My God, do you know what this would get on auction?"

"Screams of laughter. Hoots of derision. Lulu," I said, my eyes filling with tears now. "Throw in the trowel."

She glared. She ran her fingers through her thinning bangs. Then she walked back toward the hallway and I could hear her talking to the woman. I went to join them. The woman was wearing a gingham apron and had a kind, doughy face. It turned out, though, that she couldn't tell us the rabbit's price. She said to come back in a few hours when her husband was around.

The one thing I had learned well from years of watching Lulu in such situations was never to look directly at the person she was doing business with. Lulu always said that my face was too honest, and that I always gave her away. Hillary, being an actress, was of course much better at feigning indifference, and I was usually jealous of her for that. So while Lulu talked and listened, I looked at the ground and kept my eyes lowered until we were outside again.

16

I don't remember all the places we went that afternoon—all the dusty lanes and the weathered whirligigs we passed with their countless arms waving us on. We must have stopped in ten or fifteen stores. Some had very nice things that were invariably overpriced, and here Lulu would introduce herself and her gallery, give the owner her card and talk shop. But most were like the first two: indoor junkyards.

By four o'clock we were walking back along a road that hadn't led to anything, and I was exhausted. We had bought only one thing all day long: an antique tin paintbox that had hardly been a bargain but that Lulu had insisted on getting for Daddy anyway.

We were almost at the car when she stopped suddenly and turned to me with a pained look.

"I have to sit down," she said.

I didn't understand at first.

"We're almost at the car," I said.

"No, Jennifer. I have to sit down."

The car was in sight, but I stopped and turned back to her.

"Help me," she said. It was the first and only time.

"You can put your arms around me," I said. I was scared. "Look, Lulu, we're almost there."

"I have to sit down." Her voice was firm but breathy. Feeling sick myself, I helped her down to the long grass by the road.

"Look—" I began quietly, kneeling beside her.

"Don't talk," she said. A few moments later, she added, "Sorry, Jennifer. Please."

I sat down and waited. She was breathing very heavily, as she had the night she fell. There were no cars on this road. I thought about going for help, but didn't know what kind of help she needed. I wanted to know what was happening. I could only assume that her back had begun to hurt so much that it had made her feel sick or dizzy.

The sun was still strong—that Cape Cod summer light, red and orange—and it cast our shadows on the grass, stretched out like Daddy's sculptures. I remember wondering if that was where he had gotten the idea. Maybe Lulu had posed for him long ago on such an afternoon.

After a long silence, she leaned back on her elbows.

"I feel better," she said.

"Want to go?"

"In a minute."

We stayed for another fifteen or twenty, not saying anything. I hadn't been ready, and I was angry at myself for that. Then slowly she let me help her to her feet, and more slowly still we walked back to the car.

"Take a painkiller," I said.

"I did."

"When?"

"When you were buying lunch."

"Why didn't you tell me?"

She didn't say anything. I started the car. She stayed silent as we followed the trail back to the brown rabbit. I wondered if it would be the last thing she would buy.

We pulled up just as the sun began to set, a column of yellow light over the trees. Lulu didn't move. Her hands were at her sides.

"Don't you want it?" I asked.

"Yes," she said.

"Well, come *on*, then."

It was a mean thing to say. Lulu didn't answer. She just looked into my eyes, angry and pleading at the same time, and she only made me more furious. I was furious because it was all her fault. I was furious for the long day away from the house and from Daddy, who seemed to need me more. I was furious because of all the pointless stops and the hellos and the gingham ladies and the golden retrievers and the can I pet hims. And I suppose what made me most furious was the hollow sickness of the moment: sitting four yards away from a front door and a haggling session that Lulu couldn't handle.

Grimly, I said I'd do it.

"Not a penny more than forty," she said, handing me her purse.

"Do you want it or not?"

"Not a penny more than forty."

Inside the store, the woman was walking around the front room, turning off the fans. She brought the rabbit out from behind the cash register desk. It was such a preposterous-looking thing.

"My husband came and went," she said. "He told me to tell your mom seventy-five dollars. Not a penny less."

"I can't do that," I said quietly.

"That's the price."

"I can't do it," I said, suddenly realizing what I could do.

"Where's your mother, dear?" the woman asked.

"My mother," I said slowly, hating myself for it, knowing Lulu would hate me more for it, and also that she would never know, "is out in the car. She's sick, ma'am, and I have to get this for her. It means a lot to her. It means a lot to me. But I can only give you twenty dollars. Please. It's all I've got. I just have to get it for her."

"Oh dear," the gingham lady said. "She didn't *look* well, you know."

"She isn't well," I said.

She waited a long time, no doubt rehearsing what she would say to her husband later that night.

"Twenty dollars is fine, dear," she said.

I walked back to the car and presented Lulu with the rabbit. I wasn't angry any more.

"How much?" she asked me.

"Twenty dollars," I said.

"Did you talk them down?" she asked.

"Yes," I said. "They wanted seventy-five."

She beamed at me and kissed my cheek. "Now *that's* my girl," she said.

17

Jonas Irving, Lulu's doctor in Boston, had instructed her to keep a thorough record of her symptoms and the medication she took. She kept the record in a small black book, and looking back on it now makes it easier to remember the changes that began in that second week of July. Lulu still had plenty of energy and plenty of days when her symptoms seemed to disappear. But nights like the night before the party became more frequent, and she stayed closer to the house. She began to wear a bandanna to cover her thinning hair, and she sometimes stayed in bed.

The chronology of her illness is reflected in that book. In it are the facts: her loss of hunger, her nausea, the pain that she rated on a scale of one to ten and that sometimes exceeded ten; her swollen legs, swollen stomach; the bad taste from one pill, the euphoria from another. In that book, too, is the disintegration of her handwriting, increasingly shaky, less and less familiar.

In early July, though, none of us knew what was coming.

We did not know that the disease had already spread, and we were still secretly comforted by the fact that Lulu's greatest complaining seemed to come when Hillary and I didn't jump quickly enough to clear the dishes, or do the floors, or bring Daddy his coffee.

18

"Feeling better today?" Benjamin asked.

He was standing outside Harry's office, playing with an orange glow-in-the-dark yo-yo.

"What do you mean?"

"Fit as a fiddle? Ready to fly? Wait—" He held the yo-yo in his hand and raised his forefinger. "Want to see my walk-the-dog?"

"Let's fly," I said, heading for the door.

"People come from miles around to see my walk-the-dog."

I stopped and turned around.

He winked, pushed up his sleeves, but then said, "Nope. You're still sore."

"I'm *not* sore."

"You're going to be a *fine* pilot."

"I'd love to see your walk-the-dog."

He pocketed the yo-yo.

"Maybe some other time," he said.

Benjamin had fixed the vent in the plane, so the heat was

bearable this time. He had also cleaned the crumbs off the seat.

"Nice," I said, as I strapped myself in.

"The flowers?" he asked.

I followed his gaze to the back seat. A bunch of wild flowers was propped up there.

"Oh," I said. "No. No, I meant the crumbs."

"What crumbs?"

"There aren't any crumbs on the seat this week."

His grin went out like a light. "Remove the control lock," he told me.

I did.

"Check the controls."

I jockeyed the yoke back and forth and in and out.

"Vrm vrm," I said.

"We don't say 'vrm vrm.' "

"I'm terribly sorry."

"Set the wheel brakes."

I reached down and did so.

"Set the carburetor heat."

"Cold," I said.

"Set the mixture."

"Full rich."

"Good," he said.

"Set the throttle," I continued, putting it all the way in.

"No!" he shouted.

"What? What?" I asked, quickly turning it back.

"What'd you do?"

I thought. "I put it in park," I said.

"Smart girl."

And so on—through priming the engine, turning the ignition and battery on, rotating the beacon and shouting "Clear." Benjamin pushed the starter, and the prop blades began their hesitant swish. He adjusted the throttle and checked the oil pressure, and then it was my turn to taxi.

In the air, I felt no better than I had the week before. I was only beginning, I think, to resign myself to the sense of frustration and embarrassment that flying gave me. Until that summer, I had never willingly done anything that I couldn't do well. If I had seemed a success, it was because I had chosen my fields of endeavor wisely. I found my new sense of failure all the more intense because I imagined that Benjamin was loving every minute of it. I could picture him sitting around with his townie friends over a beer and talking about this spoiled rich kid who couldn't even handle straight-and-level. I had a bizarre urge to show him my photographs (see? I can do something well), but instead I just fumed and pouted and misread his concern as condescension. I shuttled back and forth between anger and embarrassment, and Benjamin never stopped grinning.

It was July 12. Lulu was visibly worse. I had taken three lessons, spent $180 of her money and knew no more about how to make a plane go down than I did about how to make it fly straight.

"Maybe I could get some books," I said to Benjamin when we had finally landed.

"Books?"

"To learn about the plane."

"*I'm* teaching you about the plane."

"No. I mean how it works."

"You want books?" he asked.

"Maybe I'd feel more in control."

"Whatever you think will help," he said.

We drove in caravan to the Sanders bookstore, the one brick building in town. We parked on Main Street about five cars away from each other.

"Well," he said, coming up next to me. "You *drive* pretty well. There may be hope."

"Oh, please."

He started to walk past me.

"Books," I said. "Flying. Remember?"

"First things first," he said. "Ice cream is one of those first things." Then he looked sheepish. "Unless you're in a hurry."

I looked more closely, expecting to see the mockery I imagined. But he was grinning shyly.

We sat on the benches outside the barbershop, half listening to the men gossip inside, furiously licking our cones before they melted in the sun.

Benjamin chatted about life on the island and life at the airport. He talked about what it had been like to grow up on an island where the summer people and all the mainlanders were hated or mistrusted.

I felt sorry for having thought he was the same. I asked him how he had turned out differently. He said he really didn't know, but it had been that way as long as he could remember. It turned out that Benjamin had been the star of his high school class—valedictorian, straight A's. He said he didn't like to fail. I smiled. He had won a scholarship to Yale, the first from Sanders in twenty-three years. He had gone to New Haven for a few semesters and had then returned, saying he didn't need it. But he was thinking about going back in the fall.

"I'm not sure why I came home," he said softly. "Maybe I got scared. Probably. I think I was starting to feel superior to all the people here. I wanted to come back before I lost my feelings for them."

"I don't think you have to *be* somewhere," I said. "If you love something you can't really lose it."

He smiled. "You really believe that," he said.

"No, not really," I told him. "But my mother does. And I'd like to," I added. "Very much."

He asked me what my childhood had been like, how it had been in an artist's family, growing up with a famous father. I wanted to explain. I told him how when I was little, and first starting to draw and paint, Daddy had taken me to his studio and shown me a color chart. He had taught me that every color had an opposite—red and green, blue and orange, yellow and purple—and that there was no such thing as pure white or pure black. Benjamin smiled encouragingly.

"I still see in blocks of color," I said.

"What do you mean?"

"Well, take those kites," I said, pointing across Main Street to the sporting goods window. "Can't you just see someone scraping them off a color chart?"

Benjamin laughed. "That would be a great job to have."

"Color-chart scraper?"

He nodded. "Every time anyone needed a color."

"I can't *believe* that you know what I mean."

"Should I be flattered or insulted?" he asked.

"Depends on what I meant when I said it."

We had finished our cones.

"Should we go?" I asked.

"No. Tell me something. Why do you really want to fly?"

The question startled me.

"I told you," I said. "It's to surprise my father."

"You hate it."

"No I don't."

"Yes," he said simply.

"Well, it's hard to explain."

"Does it mean that much to him?"

"It will," I said, suddenly remembering, suddenly wanting to draw back.

Inside the bookstore, we found the flying section and stood side by side, thumbing through all sorts of manuals and picture books. None of them had any diagrams of the works. I left Benjamin looking and walked as casually as I could over to the new arrivals section. But my book wasn't there. I went back to Benjamin.

"Could you build a plane?" I asked.

"Today?"

"I mean, do you know what makes it stay up?"

He laughed. "Of course. You do too. I've told you about the angle of the wind over the wings."

"These books don't have any diagrams."

"You like pictures?"

"I'm serious."

He grinned. "You often are."

"Where can I get some books?"

"Well, there's a real flying shop at New Bedford. We could fly there sometime. You really should get the FAA manual if you're going to stick with this."

"When?" I asked.

"Whenever. When you're a little better."

He shut the book he'd been leafing through and showed me its title: *Lift, Thrust and Drag*.

"The story," he said irresistibly, "of my relationships with women."

19

"There's this guy," I said to Hillary that night as we sat on the landing. She was lifting hand weights and sitting with her legs up against the bannister. We could hear Lulu and Daddy setting up the chess pieces down below.

"What guy?" Hillary asked.

"The guy who's giving me flying lessons."

"And?" she asked.

"And I don't know."

"Is he handsome?"

"No."

"Is he cute?"

"No."

"Sounds great," she said.

"He's really funny. He's bright. He's ambitious. He has this huge nose. We have these great talks."

"How huge is his nose?"

"Kissing him might be painful."

"How great are your talks?"

"Family," I said.

"Little Jen," she clucked.

"Oh, quiet."

"No. I think it's great. Have you slept with him yet?"

I laughed.

From downstairs, Daddy called up tensely, "Can you stop the pounding up there?"

Hillary and I looked at one another, perplexed. Then I pointed to her hand weights, which had been making a gentle clink each time she lowered them to the floor. Hillary put them down.

"Pounding?" she asked me softly.

"Sorry," I called downstairs.

Hillary lit one of my cigarettes.

"Have you slept with him?" she asked again, exhaling a thin line of smoke.

"Of course not."

"How does he kiss?"

"I haven't kissed him yet."

"Has he made a pass at you?"

"Well, not exactly," I said. "I think he bought me some wild flowers."

Hillary leaned in close. "You *think* he bought you wild flowers?"

"Stop that. It's just that he's very shy. Also I'm not very nice to him. It's hard to explain."

She smiled. "Well, you let me know the very *instant* he proposes."

Already, Lulu and Daddy were turning off the lights below. Hillary and I looked at each other apprehensively.

"Lulu? Daddy?" she called downstairs.

"Game postponed," Daddy said gruffly.

"Lulu? Are you okay?" Hillary asked.

"We're going to sleep," Daddy said. "Sleep tight, you two."

We listened as they walked toward their bedroom and closed the door.

"It'll be okay," Hillary said. I remember thinking that it was an oddly maternal thing for her to say to me, but my mind was still on Benjamin.

"How do you know, Hills?" I asked. "When someone's interested in you, I mean. How do you know?"

She shrugged. "You just do."

"That's not very helpful. You're supposed to be the big sister, you know."

"You can just tell," she said. "It's usually not too mysterious. They put their hands on your ass. Or they drool. Stuff like that. It's not too subtle."

"That doesn't sound like Benjamin," I said.

"Benjamin, huh? That's his name?"

"Benjamin Carr."

"I went out with a Benjamin once," she mused. "Gorgeous. Greek god stuff. His shoulders were so wide he looked like he was on a hanger. Lousy in bed, though. No imagination."

"Look, I happen to know that you were eighteen once too."

She laughed. "Not like you are."

Half an hour later as I got into bed, I heard Hillary walking around downstairs and then the sound of running water as she cleaned the ashtrays and coffee cups that Lulu and Daddy had used. I began to understand that she was acting a new role.

20

I thought of Benjamin the next day as Hillary and I lay in the sun. I thought of the flowers and his grin and the cool graceful manner in which he'd told me his accomplishments. I wondered if he really liked me or if he was just being polite. I realized I cared what he thought of me, and I tried to force him out of my mind. Lulu and Daddy, I thought. I would wait on the blue bench and the plane would take off and I would never see them again.

It was three o'clock. Daddy had worked in the morning and come back up to the house for a swim with Lulu. No problem with that, Dr. Irving had said. Good for her to get exercise.

Daddy's cries for help mingled with the cries of the gulls, and Hillary and I, lazing in the sun, did not understand, at first, what was happening.

By the time we reached the beach, running as fast as we could down the long staircase, Daddy had already pulled

Lulu from the water. They were lying side by side on the shore, panting and sandy.

"What happened?" Hillary and I shouted together, running toward them. They were too winded to answer, and at some point in the frozen moment waiting to hear their voices, Hillary and I reached for each other. We figured that out hours later, when we both found small red welts where our nails had dug into each other's hands.

"A cramp in her back," Daddy finally managed to say.

"Lulu?" Hillary said to her, kneeling beside her, efficient, ready to help.

"She couldn't swim," Daddy continued. His eyes filled with tears. "She started to sink."

I realized that I couldn't move. I was standing perhaps five yards from Lulu and I was scared of her, scared that she would get sick, or pass out, or scream in pain. It wasn't until she sat up and forced a smile that she was Lulu again and I could draw closer. It was the same as the night she had fallen. She had ceased to be Lulu, and in some strange way that I did not understand then and am only beginning to understand now, I ceased to be me as well. This was the reality I had been waiting for, and I found myself completely unequipped to deal with it.

She could not quite straighten up and so we supported her from three sides, nearly carrying her up the stairs back to the house. We put her in bed, wet bathing suit and all, because she did not want us to have to change her clothes for her. I was relieved, and ashamed of my relief.

She smiled at Daddy and reached for his hand.

"Scared me," he said.

"Nothing to be scared of."

After she had fallen asleep, I walked back down to the beach. The sun was throwing an electric current of light across the waves, so bright it had no color. I stared at the spot where she might have died, and at the beach, where I had been unable to help her.

I imagined myself as a helpless infant with soiled clothes. I imagined all the messy intimate moments: Lulu teaching me to blow my nose, scrape my teeth, clean my ears, get sick. She had done the same for Hillary. Our bodies and smells and illnesses had not repelled her. We had been, somehow, an extension of her. And I could not, at least not yet, summon the same courage for her. I wanted to be far away so she wouldn't see my fear, and I knew she'd already seen it.

I went back to the house after the sun set. Lulu was still asleep. Hillary drove to town with Daddy, and for the first time in my life I was afraid to be alone with my mother. I sat at the living room table, avoiding my reflection in the glass and praying that she would not wake up needing something I couldn't give.

21

Families do not have to be large to be confusing. In small close families like mine, the confusion comes from the variety of roles each member can play, and from the strong memory of old alliances and hurts. I had always secretly envied Hillary her similarity to Lulu. I had envied the sunny ease of her conversations. Lulu never had to tell Hillary "Just because." But Hillary had always envied my long talks with Daddy. It wasn't as simple as Hillary and Lulu or Daddy and me, though. I had something with Lulu. I was trying to do a lot of the things she had wanted to do at my age. And Hillary had something with Daddy. She could be a second Lulu far more easily than I.

Watching Hillary's frank and perfect behavior with Lulu on the beach had made me jealous. When I woke the next morning and found them laughing together in the kitchen I didn't even say good morning. I set out for Daddy's studio.

He must have sensed that I needed something, because he let me sit with him while he worked. He had started to paint the second horse. I picked up a book that was lying near the worktable, and I settled back against the wall. I saw pictures of horses by Dentzel and Carmel and Looff—the greatest carousel carvers of all. They had made their fame right after the turn of the century. Dentzel, I read in one caption, employed thirty or forty people to turn out five or six carousels a year. I told this to Daddy.

"Really," he said, without much interest.

"Five a *year,* Daddy."

"Yes."

"Well, how's this going to be ready in time?" I asked.

"In time for what?"

"In time for Lulu to see it, of course."

He looked at me as if the thought had never crossed his mind. I felt another stab of pity for him.

"I don't know," he said vaguely.

"Dentzel had assistants," I said. "Just like the old masters."

Daddy dipped a new paintbrush in a jar of pink.

"I'm going to give them names," he said.

"What?"

"The horses. I'm naming them. Want to guess who this one is?"

Baffled, I looked at the horse he was working on.

"Bob," he said. "This one is Bob Reese."

I looked again. I smiled. The horse's eyes did have Bob's kind of half-closed look.

"Nice," I said. "Daddy. What about Dentzel?"

"What?"

"Dentzel had workmen. Let me be your workman."

"Oh, Jen."

"Really. I wouldn't get in the way. I'd keep you company. I want to help."

"I don't think so, darling."

"I could help you paint. I could buy your supplies.

Anything." He didn't seem to understand the need to hurry. His intensity didn't seem related to time.

"What about your own work?" he asked, just as he had a few weeks before.

"I don't know," I said. "I want to help you."

"I'll have to think about it," he said.

I spent the morning with him. I studied the Herschell-Spillman zebra with its head thrown back, the black Muller "jumper" with the bright red and white bridle, the Philadelphia Toboggan Company giraffe, nearly six feet tall. I learned that the spectator side of a carousel horse was called the romance side. I learned that a carousel horse attached at the top was called a Flying Jenny. I told these things to Daddy, made some suggestions, then let him work in silence. But I did not understand that he was not making a gift: I didn't know that he was trying to make something live.

22

On July 19, the next Wednesday, Benjamin and I had been up in the air for about half an hour. He was trying to teach me the three kinds of motion: pitch, roll and yaw. He was being charming. Pitch, he said, was like a rocking horse. Roll was tilting side to side, like a tightrope walker's arms. Yaw was steering.

"Vrm vrm," he said, showing me yaw.

"So I guess," I said tentatively, "that if you lost control of one you'd still be able to fly."

He laughed over the headset.

"You definitely need all three" was all he said. Then he tapped the altimeter. We had dropped altitude.

"Bring her up," he said.

I looked at him.

"Bring her *up,*" he repeated. But I pulled back too hard on the yoke, and the nose flew up before me.

"Take it," I said as I felt us climbing and heard the engine noise growing thinner.

He held his hands up, away from his yoke.

"Benjamin," I said. "Take it."

Quietly, he said, "You know how to fix this."

"Please, Benjamin."

"Do it."

"Please."

"Just do it."

I tried to push in on the yoke, but I was too timid and too late. The plane stalled out, and I screamed. It was like going over a roller coaster. The nose pointed almost straight down now, and all I could see was the blue ocean and a single sailboat the size of a toy.

I let go of the yoke completely. In the split second before Benjamin took the controls, I saw fury and frustration in his face. It was just like Daddy shouting "You've got an eye."

Then Benjamin was in charge. Silently he brought us out of the spin and started the engine again. We climbed back up to three thousand feet, and then he turned us neatly around. I felt sick and embarrassed, but I told him that I didn't want to go back.

He laughed lightly, looking out the window for other planes.

"Benjamin," I said. "The hour's not up yet." Lulu, I thought. The end of the summer.

"Come on, Jennifer."

"I want to learn to fly," I said.

"I think we should talk about this."

"Later."

"This doesn't make any sense," he said.

"Let me turn her around," I said. "I can do it."

"No."

"Benjamin."

"No!"

"Look—" I began.

"I'm going to land," he said.

We came in a little fast. I could tell he was upset.

"Come on," he said, opening my door. I sat very still, staring at the rain streaks the sun lighted on the window. My knees were trembling.

"Come on," he said more gently. "Don't be a baby."

"Don't be mad at me," I said.

"I'm not mad at you."

"I want to learn to fly."

"I know. I just want to talk to you. Come on."

I followed him, my head down, to the wood fence by the gate. We climbed up on it and sat side by side.

"Tell me," he said, "why you really want this. You know you're not a pilot."

"I want to be."

"Well, I know that. I'm trying to find out why."

I knocked my feet against the fence and waited for the image of Daddy wading out of the ocean alone to go away. I felt lonely and I wanted to tell Benjamin about Lulu. He thought he was starting to know me, that we were starting to be friends.

"I can't tell you now," I said. "But just give me one more chance. I don't like to fail any more than you do."

Tentatively, he said, "I saw this book of yours."

"What?"

"I saw this book of yours. At the Sanders bookstore. You didn't tell me you'd done a book."

I shrugged.

"I thought it was wonderful," he said. "If you can do that, why do you need to do this?"

"Just give me one more chance," I said.

23

On the way home, I stopped across the street from the bookstore and sat for a while, summoning the courage to go inside. Finally, I could see the place emptying out and could tell it was about to close. I slipped inside. My book was sitting on the new arrivals table. There were ten or twelve copies of it. I thought about buying one for Lulu and Daddy, but I didn't have the nerve. Anyway, I thought, I had already given it to them. I needed something new to give.

24

Benjamin called that night to ask if I was all right.

"Fine," I said.

"Are you sure?"

"Yes."

"I was worried about you today. You looked so upset."

"I know. I'm sorry."

"Don't be sorry."

"I'm embarrassed."

"I know. Sometimes it's like that."

There was a long pause.

"Benjamin?" I asked.

"I don't understand you," he said. "But I'd like to."

I laughed. "So would I," I said.

"I'm going to give you two more lessons," he said, "and after that we'll see."

"Thank you, Benjamin."

"Don't thank me. I have an ulterior motive."

I repeated the conversation to Hillary later that evening.

We were sitting on the landing as usual. I told her I wasn't sure if Benjamin was like this with everyone or just with me. Hillary finally flipped back a strand of her hair and said:

"Oh, Jen, come on."

When I started to protest, she stood up and bent over to touch her toes, her legs perfectly straight and brown, her blond hair sweeping lightly against the polished wood floor.

"Why don't you just *do* it?" she said.

25

"Who do you think was the best?" I asked Daddy. I was perched on top of Bob, whom Daddy had finished. Carved seashells, reminiscent of the beach Bob loved and painted, outlined the saddle. I was leaning backward against the neck.

"The best carver or the best carousel man?" Daddy asked.

"You think there's a difference?"

"Sure."

He was bending over Pillari, the third horse in the series. The legs hadn't been carved yet. Pillari was going to be pink and white, very slender, but with an incredible stretch—six feet in all. He was going to wear a bow tie (as Joe did), and his saddle was going to be trimmed with wood carved to look like an ornate picture frame.

"Is it going to move?" I asked.

Daddy blew some sawdust from Pillari's eye. "The carousel?"

"Will we be able to ride it?"

"No." He laughed. "Do you know what that would cost?"

"Sam could do it."

"There are some things even Sam can't do."

"Do you know something about Lulu that you're not telling us?"

"Why would you think that?"

"I don't know. You're just so private."

"Not as private as she is."

"Are you scared?"

"Oh, Jen."

"Are you, Dad? Are you scared?"

He looked up at me. "Of course I'm scared," he said.

He waited a long time.

"Does she talk to you, Jen?"

"About it, you mean?" I asked.

"Yes."

"I wish she did."

"I keep thinking I should tell her that I wish it wasn't happening."

"She doesn't talk to you?"

"No."

"She knows we love her."

"Hand me that blade."

I hopped off the horse and brought the tool to him.

"Let me paint something," I said.

"Maybe later."

26

A horse farm had answered Lulu's ad. Sam drove out Saturday morning to pick up a truckload of the white daisies that grew wild in the field where the horses ran. The farm had said Lulu could have as many as she could take away. Free. No charge at all, they said. Lulu glowed as if she had known it all along.

Somewhat trampled, slightly anemic, they arrived in Sam's truck at around eleven. Hillary, Sam and I put them in the ground as Lulu looked on from a lawn chair, triumphant.

"Some of them are gone already," Hillary told her.

"That's all right," Lulu said, and she showed us how to spread their seeds, crumpling the yellow stamens gently between her fingers. I only found out recently that you can't spread a daisy's seeds that way.

We must have put more than a hundred in the soil, Lulu directing us to form an arc around the lawn. As I worked I regretted that she had not taught me more about gardening. I wondered what would happen to the garden, to the house.

But as we worked I saw Daddy sneak up from the road, a finger to his lips, a twinkle in his eye. Lulu hadn't seen him.

In Daddy's hand was a perfect wooden rabbit, which he placed discreetly among the beach plum bushes on the lawn's periphery. Hillary saw him too and smiled, delighted. I was less so. I couldn't imagine why he would take time away from her carousel. But he just sneaked back to the side and stood by a tree, waiting, impish and beaming.

He didn't have long to wait. When Lulu stood up to inspect our work, she spotted the rabbit right away.

"Look!" she cried.

The rabbit didn't move.

"What?" Hillary asked nonchalantly.

"The rabbit! Look at him! He's just waiting there!" Lulu said, pointing.

"What rabbit?" Hillary asked.

"Hillary! Jennifer?"

I took a few steps toward the edge of the lawn.

"I don't see any rabbit, Lulu," I said.

"Girls!" And then she figured it out. She looked from Hillary to me and back to the rabbit. Then she started laughing.

"Where is he? Where is my husband?"

Daddy pranced out from behind the tree like the boy she let him be.

"Gotcha, Kate," he said. "Gotcha." He did a little two-step in front of her. I looked on, amazed. Where had he managed to find this delight? But I laughed too. We all laughed. Even Sam had a good chuckle.

Lulu told Daddy to go back to work, but she wasn't fooling anyone. We could tell that she was smitten. Forty-eight years old and married more than twenty-five years, and she looked better than Hillary with Spencer.

Daddy kissed her and took the road to his studio. Hillary

asked for my laundry—Lulu again. Sam winked and drove off, and Lulu stood, euphoric, surrounded by her flowers. She led me on a tour of the garden as if neither of us had ever seen it before. She pointed to a patch of zinnias that had just come in. They were new and very beautiful: bright red and orange, small suns. I asked Lulu to give me one.

"You're going to press it, aren't you?" she asked, a hand on her hip and the sun across her face.

I looked at her, startled. I had always pressed flowers, and she had always chosen the flowers for me to press when I asked for one.

"Of course," I said, looking down, speaking softly. "Like always," I said.

Lulu knelt down stiffly. Resolutely, she snipped off one of the prettiest ones. I still have it. But that was, I realized as she handed the flower to me, the difference between us. Lulu would never have considered pressing a flower. She simply didn't need to and she never had. My doing so was, to her, a kind of crime.

Lulu had the gift of knowing that the zinnias would come in again the next summer, just as bright and beautiful, maybe even more so. She knew she wouldn't have to remember them, because they would always be there at her reach. Lulu needed to save nothing: she needed no flowers, no photographs, no proof, no evidence. She had the future harbored within her the way I harbored the past.

27

Benjamin called Wednesday morning to say I should come early to the lesson.

"Why?"

"Field trip," he said. "I thought we'd go to New Bedford and get a book for you."

"What about your other lessons?"

"Canceled."

"For me?"

"Well, let me check," he said. "You are Jennifer Burke, right?"

I laughed. "That was very nice of you," I said.

"I know."

"Tell me. Have you been this nice all along?"

"Nicer."

"I'll see you at one," I said.

28

I drove by the church on the way to the airport.

CHILDREN DON'T CARE WHAT YOU KNOW
UNTIL THEY KNOW THAT YOU CARE

Not in this family, I thought. But I would not have wanted to change that then.

In the airport parking lot, I was just about to get out of the car when Benjamin drove up in a big red van. He didn't see me, and he parked across the lot. A wire fence separated him from Oscar, just across the way, and I watched him walk up to it, glance around, then quickly climb over it. Something in his manner kept me watching from a distance.

He unlocked Oscar's cabin and looked around inside. A few moments later he scaled the fence again and returned to the van. Still looking around, he unloaded a huge wicker basket and a quilt. Walking faster now, he went down to the end of the fence, through the swinging door and back to the plane. After putting the things inside, he tucked his T-shirt into his blue jeans and sprinted for the fresh grass beyond the tie-downs. He emerged several moments later with a bunch of wild flowers. I saw my hands on the steering wheel. They looked like Lulu's hands. Benjamin ran now to the plane and stowed the flowers. I smiled and ran my fingers through my bangs.

We decided that he would fly us to New Bedford, and I would fly us back.

The new Bedford terminal was much larger than the one at Sanders, and even more tacky. Large glass cases advertised local stores with displays of golfing equipment, water skis and bathroom fixtures. A deserted row of pinball machines blinked red and white and gaudy. Vending machines offered soft drinks, candy, coffee and sandwiches.

"Hey, look," Benjamin said, walking up to an old machine. Starbright Vacations, it said, in fifties lettering, like the kind in Lulu's college yearbook. It showed combs, shampoo, toothpaste, key rings, shower caps, soap, shaving cream, razors. Each object was mounted on a circle of horribly faded colored paper.

"Those colors must have been scraped off a long time ago," Benjamin said.

"Let's buy something."

"Need a shampoo?" he asked.

"No, look," I said, and pointed to a circle with "Tricks and Toys" printed inside it. There were rings and a tiny jigsaw puzzle and miniature books.

"Terrific," he said, reaching into his pocket.

"My treat," I said.

I put a quarter in the machine and pulled the handle. Out came a small flat white box the shape of a candy bar. I handed it to him.

"For you," I said solemnly.

"You don't even know what it is."

"Sure I do. It's a trick or a toy."

He opened it, grinning, and pulled out six white cards with numbers printed all over them. I started to laugh.

"What is it?" I asked.

He read the instructions silently.

"Pick a card," he said, arranging them before me. It was a numbers game that allowed him to know what number I had chosen from one of the cards.

"How'd you do that?" I asked him.

"It's magic," he said.

"Benjamin."

So he explained the way the trick worked, the ordering of the numbers. It was based on a principle I've long since forgotten.

"How do you know about this?" I asked.

"I studied it in applied math."

I was delighted. The things he knew were real.

We had a hard time pulling ourselves away from that machine. We stayed, laughing, while the waiting passengers looked away, embarrassed. Finally we had used up all our quarters, and my handbag was filled with fake chocolates, exploding bubble gum, more magic number cards and a tiny joke book. There was a ring that squirted water, which Benjamin insisted that I fill in the water fountain.

"Now what?" I asked.

"Wear it," he said. "Just in case I get out of line."

We found the flying shop around the back of the terminal. He ordered a copy of the official FAA manual for me.

"You'll need to memorize this," he said, "if you take your written exam."

"*When.*"

"Right."

We walked outside. I would find the answer in that book, I thought. It had been cloudy off and on all day. Now we stood by the terminal building, which was shingled and weathered like the one on Sanders. The sun spilled like a varnish over the planes and the grass.

"Are you hungry?" Benjamin asked. "I brought some food."

"A little," I said, which was a lie. I wasn't hungry at all.

He went over to Oscar and came back with the quilt, which he spread ceremoniously on the grass, bending to straighten out each corner and to smooth out each wrinkle. I sat down, feeling the prickly dry grass beneath the blanket under my legs, remembering childhood picnics by the puppet pond with Lulu. Benjamin made another trip to the plane and returned with the basket. He pulled out a thermos and cups and cold cuts and fresh bread and cake. But he had not brought the flowers. They had to be for me, I thought.

"Sandwich?" Benjamin asked me.

"Sure."

I decided that I was in love with him.

I met his eyes just long enough to give him no doubt about why I was meeting his eyes. Stand up, I thought, and walk over to that plane and reach for my flowers and give them to me. Which is exactly what he did.

On the way home, he turned on the automatic pilot and we kissed for the first time. Benjamin's hands were huge and strong, and they cupped around my face and neck, making me safe, encircled, and the first thing he said when he stopped kissing me was "I think I've fallen in love with you."

AUGUST

1

Benjamin and I never got to our lesson the next time. We went instead to the Scavenger, a seedy bar off the airport road, that was draped with fishing nets and sinister red lamps. The Scavenger had an old jukebox with burnt-out lights and about ten records. It had no curfew and opened at noon. It attracted the island's toughest clientele. I had only been there once. It was not a place where a blond summer girl could just pop in on her own.

Benjamin led me in proudly, saying hello to a few of the regulars at the bar, introducing me to Greg, the bartender.

We sat in one of the wooden booths where pilots and, before them, fishermen had carved their names in the table. Benjamin told me about Mory's at Yale. We asked Greg for two Cokes, and we smoked cigarettes and sat there for five and a half hours. Talking to Benjamin was effortless, like talking to Hillary or Lulu or Daddy. It had never occurred to me that there might be a person who was not a Burke but who shared that rather embarrassing Burke assumption: that life was somehow waiting for us to shape it; that we were special; that we could give more.

Quietly, Benjamin told me that he wanted to be a writer.

"I've always gone through things very fast," he said. "I learn a lot about them, and then I lose interest." He gave a light laugh and cocked his head to the right. I thought of asking him if that meant women, too. I looked at his eyes and he looked right back at mine. But then he shrugged. "Anyway," he said, "writing is the one thing you can never really get tired of. You can never really win at it."

"Photography," I suggested, thinking of all the recent pictures that I hadn't tried to take.

"Of course," he said. "Right. Maybe anything you make."

Benjamin's parent's, he told me, were both dead, and that had a lot to do with his wanting to stay on Sanders Island. His mother had died when he was six. He said he could only remember one thing about her: the way the locket on her gold chain used to swing into his hands when she bent over to give him a bath or tuck him in at night. He still had the locket, he said, and he showed it to me, a shiny gold oval hanging from his key ring. He told me he had kept her silverware, too, which had been her only dowry. He blamed his father for his mother's death. Herbie Carr had died an alcoholic when Benjamin was sixteen. He had kept nothing of his father's.

Benjamin said his greatest fear was that he'd end up like his parents. I said my greatest fear was that I wouldn't end up like mine.

A scratched forties recording of "String of Pearls" was playing on the jukebox. Its rhythm gave me courage.

"Who taught you?" I asked.

"What do you mean?"

"Who taught you to be the way you are?"

He smiled, flattered. "Well," he said shyly, "I guess the good things in me come from Harry. He's my family."

"I thought Harry Chambers was just a hardened old bachelor."

Benjamin laughed. "Oh, he is. And he'd be thrilled to hear you put it just that way."

"Are you going to be a hardened old bachelor, too? With an airport of your own?" I teased.

Benjamin took the heel of his Coke glass and industriously blended all the little water droplets into one big water droplet.

"Well, as far as the airport goes, no way. How many pilots do you think have read Proust?"

I laughed. "That's just the kind of thing my father would say."

He smiled but kept his eyes down, still playing with the glass.

"As to the other thing," he said. "I don't know if it comes from Harry or not, but I guess after a while you see all your friends falling in love and breaking up, and you see how tough it is to make something work, to be sincere. You just stop believing that what they talk about is real."

The jukebox had stopped. There was a burst of laughter from the bar.

"I warn you," I said. "I have a terrific tendency to be sincere."

"So do I, actually," he said. "It's one of my shortcomings." He looked up and grinned.

"Shouldn't you be getting back to your lessons?" I asked, glancing at my watch.

"I canceled them," he said. "Thunderstorms."

His eyes were as gray as Daddy's were blue. His eyes were like mosaic floors, with a thousand little facets. I told him about Lulu and Daddy. I told him about their swims on the beach, their games of chess, their Scotches at sunset. I told him about Lulu posing for Daddy and Daddy sketching for Lulu, how they lived for each other, how they were part of one unit, inseparable, locked.

"Oh, come on," he said. "Nothing's that perfect. There must be things they don't show you."

"That's just Harry talking."

"I've never loved anyone."

"I know."

"I don't know if I can," he said.

"Of course you can," I told him, with missionary warmth. I was Lulu.

He laughed again, more softly now. "What makes *you* so sure?"

"Because everyone can," I said, wondering if I really believed it, but loving the way it sounded and the way it made me seem. "It's the only thing that makes any sense. It's the only thing that really lasts. It makes everything fall into place."

He said I spoke of it as if it were something you could pick up and hold. I said I thought of it that way.

"And you either feel it or you don't?" he asked.

"That's right."

"Yes or no? Black or white?"

"Some things just *are*," I said.

"I thought there was no such thing as a pure black or a pure white," he said.

"You're very clever."

"That's another one of my shortcomings."

The bar filled with people as the rain began to fall outside. The jukebox scratched and whined, and our ashtray was filled with cigarette butts.

I told Benjamin about Spencer and Hillary. I told him I had a crush on a blond runner named Jim. He told me he had just broken up with a thirty-four-year-old nurse named Suzanne.

"That must have been rough," I said.

"Not really."

"Didn't it hurt you to hurt her?"

"I didn't hurt her."

"I don't believe you."

"Really." He paused, his gray eyes suddenly dark. "All the women I've gone out with are still my friends."

"How do you manage that?" I asked.

"I think it's simple," he said. "I think I never give anything that I can't take back."

"That isn't love," I said.

"I know."

2

It was dark when we left the Scavenger, and I drove home in the rain humming "String of Pearls."

The lights were off in Lulu's room, but she was awake when I tiptoed in.

"Couldn't you sleep?" I asked.

"For a while."

"Where's Daddy?"

"Working, I hope."

"Where's Hillary?"

"Doing the laundry."

"Again?"

"Rub my back?" she asked.

I looked in the black book on her night table. She had listed the pain as only a two.

"You're feeling better," I said.

"Much."

The rain pounded on the roof and streamed down the windows. We could hear the thunder, and the lightning lit the beach and the ocean. I braced myself on my left elbow and helped Lulu roll over. I started with her neck and worked my way down to her lower back. Then I began again. From time to time, without breaking my rhythm, I would lean forward slightly and kiss her cheek.

"Remember when you were a little girl and you were afraid of the lightning?" she asked. "We used to let you sleep with us."

"Daddy snored."

"He still does. A little lower," she said.

"Tomorrow I'm going to take your birthday photograph," I said.

"I don't think so."

"But your birthday."

"Not important."

"But Lulu."

"Look at me." It was the closest she had come, or ever would, to self-pity.

"You look beautiful."

"I do not look beautiful."

She was right, of course. She did not look beautiful at all, and I realized that anyone seeing her for the first time that summer would have been appalled. There was a yellowish tint to her skin that made her look waxy and tense. She had covered her head with a blue bandanna, but I noticed that her hairline was gone. Her stomach was slightly swollen, and her arms and neck were painfully thin.

"Sing to me," she said.

"What should I sing?"

"You know. That one I like."

Them that's got shall get
Them that's not shall lose
So the Bible says
And it still is news:

Mama may have, and Papa may have
But God bless the child
That's got his own. . . .

"I like the way you sing," Lulu said.

"That's because you're tone-deaf."

She laughed.

"Mom?"

"What?"

"Is that song about you or me?"

"Oh, honestly, Jennifer."

"Really."

"Well," she said, "I suppose it's about both of us."

My hand slipped and went too hard on her lower back. She winced.

"Did I hurt you?"

"No," she said.

Then Hillary walked in, carrying an armload of fresh towels.

"Oh," she said tightly, depositing the towels on Lulu's dresser. "*You're* here."

"Perceptive," I said.

"I'm putting the towels right here, Lulu," she said. She did a sharp turn and left the room.

"Why don't you help her with more of the chores?" Lulu asked.

"She hasn't asked me to."

"That's no reason."

"I think she likes it."

"You should help her anyway. Is the rain coming in through the windows?"

I stood up and looked.

"No," I said, walking back to the bed. "Mom?" I asked, settling down beside her again. "How did you know about Daddy?"

"I just knew."

"Did you know that he'd be a success? Was that it?"

"Oh no," she said, and laughed. "I would have loved him anyway."

"Why?"

"Just because," she said. "I just liked being with him." She smiled. "I loved being with him."

"You know the pilot we saw at the airport?" I asked. "I like being with him."

"I know."

"Hillary *told* you?"

"Yes."

"You can't keep a secret in this family," I said, thinking of the one I would have to keep.

"Just take it slowly, Jen," she said.

"I will. But he makes me laugh."

"Maybe that's his funny nose."

I hugged her. "She told you that too?"

"I want to sit up."

I rolled her onto her back, and she rested there a few minutes. Then I rolled her toward me, tucking my hands under her arms, pulling forward. I was only a little less frightened of her, only a little more sure.

Lulu put her head against my neck, the way I had with her the night of the party, the day of the plane ride, all my life.

Her head was hot, and I stroked her forehead.

"You know," I said, "you're taking this very well."

3

Upstairs, the rain was even louder. I found Hillary in her bedroom, putting clothes away.

"Some storm, huh?" I said.

"Get out."

"What do you mean, get out?"

"Get out."

"You're angry."

"Now you're being perceptive."

"What is it?"

"You don't do a thing around here."

"That's not true," I said.

She glared.

"I have things to do," I said.

"Flying lessons," she said scornfully. "And never-never land with Daddy."

"Daddy needs me."

"Lulu needs you."

"You're just jealous because he's letting me help," I said.

"Lulu says she can tell that you're scared."

I sat on the edge of her bed. I hated her.

"You're just saying that."

"It's true."

"Well," I said, "you act like you're the only one who knows how to do anything."

"I have things to do too, you know. I've got the reading in a week."

"You know that part by heart," I said. Which was true. She had it down.

"That's not the point," she said.

"You took over," I said. "I thought you wanted to."

No response.

"You don't let me near the kitchen when you're cooking," I said. Which was also true. But that wasn't the point either.

"Get out," she said, and I did.

The point was that she needed someone to fight with who could fight back. The point was that she needed to be angry at something that she could change.

4

The next morning I was in the kitchen before Hillary woke up. I emptied the dishwasher and the dish drain, and I cleaned out the refrigerator, bringing a large bag of trash down to the road. It was so foggy that I couldn't even see the puppet pond through the trees. Sanders got like that after heavy rains, socked in and quiet, the blues and greens both gray.

Back at the house, I made fresh coffee, squeezed fresh orange juice, made a pitcher of lemonade and boiled some eggs. That was about the extent of my culinary talents then. No one drank the lemonade. But Hillary thanked me for the orange juice. We were no longer equals. She *had* taken on Lulu's role as head of the household. But I wanted to make peace with her, and later in the day offered to finish her portfolio. She wasn't interested. She said she had more important things to do. She said she was thinking about canceling her audition, but I told her she had to do it, for the same reason that Daddy had to be in his studio: because Lulu wanted us to go on as we'd been. So Hillary said she'd go to Boston, but she said she'd only be gone a day.

5

Some time during that first week in August, Lulu had called Dr. Irving with an update on her symptoms. It was typical of her not to have Daddy or one of us serve as a go-between; she wanted to know everything that was happening to her.

The doctor had said she should have some more tests done, to see if the growth had stopped or spread. So on Friday morning, Daddy, Hillary and I drove Lulu to the Sanders Medical Center, just another shingled house on Beach Street. Hillary and I did the grocery shopping while Daddy waited with Lulu. I had tried to convince him to stay home and work, but he had insisted on coming along.

They were standing together at the front door when Hillary and I pulled up. Lulu was wearing her long beige cashmere cardigan and her denim skirt. Daddy had on his suede jacket, his jeans and his red flannel shirt. They looked like a thousand snapshots I'd taken. He had his arm around her, and she was leaning against his shoulder.

"Look at them," Hillary said, and I was startled by the sadness in her voice, an admission even more sobering than her role as Lulu. "God," she said. "Look at his face."

"I know."

"I hate this," she said.

"I know."

We switched to the back seats as Lulu and Daddy climbed in front.

"He'll call us with the results this afternoon," Lulu said before we could even ask her.

No one said anything as we drove down the long curve of Beach Street. Lulu had her hand on the back of the front seat. Hillary, typically, had one hand around her own hair to keep it from the wind.

"What do you see?" Daddy said.

No one wanted to play.

"Come on. What do you see?" he demanded.

Reluctantly, I closed my eyes and turned toward the ocean, feeling the sun on my face.

"Lighthouse," I said.

"Right."

"Bushes," Hillary said, with little more spirit.

"Right. You too, kid," Daddy told Lulu.

"All right, then," she said, and as I opened my eyes I saw her turn, with some difficulty, toward the water. The sun crossed her face like a beacon, and she raised her chin just slightly, waiting. The beach stretched on for miles. We were on the way back to the house. It took a few minutes before any shadow passed over the sun.

Daddy, being playful, tried to fool her by taking a shortcut through the woods. She wasn't fooled.

"Home," she said.

6

Dr. Irving called around six o'clock. The doctors at the Medical Center had called him, apparently squeamish about dealing directly with Lulu. Her back, he told Daddy, was better. But the cancer had spread to her liver, and that was not good, he said. Dr. Irving did not tell Daddy that there was a lot of hope. Nor did he say three months, six months or a year. In fact, while no one ever said she would live, no one said she would die either.

What Dr. Irving did say was that she should continue to take the chemotherapy and radiation, and he set a date in Boston, August 26, for her next treatment.

After Daddy had told her, and she had told us, and we had asked Daddy privately if there was more she wasn't telling, Lulu insisted on making dinner. She asked both Hillary and me to help, and she showed us her secret recipe for Hungarian goulash—Daddy's favorite. She was matter-of-fact, even cheerful. Hillary matched her smile for smile.

At dinner, we took turns prompting Hillary on her lines.

Afterwards, Lulu complained that we were slow in clearing the table and then said the coffee was weak.

"And look at these dishes," she said, coming into the kitchen to get an ashtray once she and Daddy had begun a game of chess. "Is this your idea of clean?"

Hillary and I stared in disbelief, then realized she was serious.

"Sorry, Lulu."

"Sorry, Lulu."

"Sorry isn't good enough. If you're going to do something, then do it right or don't do it at all. How many times have I told you that?"

"Don't yell," Hillary said.

"Clean up this *mess!*" Lulu shouted. "Do you want *me* to do it?" She stormed out of the kitchen.

Hillary threw her sponge into the sink.

"Doesn't she know?" she asked, nearly in tears. "Doesn't she know how much I've been doing around here? Every meal. The dishes. The laundry. I've given her the pills, I've stayed up with her, I've watered the lawn. I've even chased her damned rabbits. Doesn't she know?"

"Of course she knows," I said. "I think that's the point."

7

Sithwell's Bay is a fishing village, the first that was settled on Sanders Island and the least touched by tourism. It is a town built backward from the spine of a long wooden dock, where fishing vessels from around the world have come into port. There was still only one restaurant there the summer I met Benjamin, and it had always been there, along with the country store that sold penny candy, the liquor store and drugstore. Benjamin had grown up in Sithwell's Bay, in a house on a hill overlooking the harbor, with a long steep staircase leading down to the dock.

"Eighty-four stairs," he told me when we went to visit the next day. "I counted them a hundred times when I was a little boy."

Benjamin told me that his father had built those stairs, and the large gray house they led to. He had been a ship's carpenter, repairing the boats that came into the harbor. Benjamin told me he didn't think much about his father or mother, and I didn't believe him.

He took my hand as we walked.

I had been to Sithwell's Bay many times before, but had always felt like an outsider. Lulu and Daddy had taken Hillary and me there when we were little because they loved the small restaurant on the dock that served clams on the half shell and pitchers of martinis. Lulu and Daddy would find a table on the restaurant's porch, and Hillary and I would sit on the dock, eating fish and chips and feeding the French fries to the big friendly dogs that were always around.

In more recent summers I had driven to Sithwell's Bay alone—usually at dusk—when I was sad or when I was looking for good light to shoot by. Everything always seemed very sharp and clear out there: the white sails against the deep blue harbor; the web of crossed lines and moorings; the pulled-up anchors in silhouette; the wooden pilings where the gulls sat like carvings.

"Can we go up to the house?" I asked.

"No."

"Why not?"

"Because I don't know who lives there now."

We walked out toward the end of the dock. The sky was peach and the water was gray. The wind picked up. Benjamin put his arm around me. At the end of the dock, we sat together and dangled our legs. I could hear the splash of the water against the hulls of the boats behind us, and the gulls and terns circling the piles of empty shells outside the restaurant. I could feel my heart racing and feel the afternoon sun still on Benjamin's shirt.

"Are you ashamed of your parents?" I asked him.

"Yes."

"You know I don't care."

"I know."

"It must hurt."

"It's old."

"Still."

"It fades," he said.

It shouldn't, I thought.

"You forget," he said. "You just do."

I hugged him very hard and kissed his neck gently. I wanted to tell him about Lulu, but I didn't need to yet.

8

Spencer was flying down that evening for a dance at the island's yacht club. Benjamin told me he'd meet the three of us there. But I knew how awkward it would be for him to be a guest where all his childhood friends were working as waiters.

"Don't bother with the dance," I told him as we pulled up to the VW, which I'd left in the airport lot. "Just meet us at the dock near the beach around ten thirty."

I sped home, all the quiet grace of the evening giving way to excitement and nerves. I took a quick shower and put on some lipstick and eyeliner that Hillary had left in the bathroom. And I tried on every dress in my closet, running downstairs to show Lulu each one. She finally approved a simple white cotton sundress.

"He's probably an old-fashioned boy," she said.

The dance was interminable. I stayed in a corner of the darkened room, watching intently as the turning mirrored ball threw light and shadows on the ceilings and walls and sliding glass doors. Standing close to the bar at one point, I could hear the two bartenders and one of the waiters jeering at all the pretty people in their blazers and pastels, and I wanted to be with Benjamin, to be on his side. As usual, Hillary and Spencer seemed fascinated by each other, Spencer smiling an extravagant smile, Hillary blond and sultry, wearing an old pink strapless cocktail dress of Lulu's. She looked beautiful and she knew it, but for once I enjoyed her flirtation. Benjamin, I thought. I did not think of Lulu.

Ten thirty finally came, and I tapped Hillary's shoulder. The three of us walked down the boardwalk to the pier. I could tell they were a little drunk.

Benjamin was already there. He had exchanged his blue jeans and T-shirt for khakis and a blue blazer. He stood against a horizon of the far shore's little lights, and he hugged me, shaking Hillary's and Spencer's hands with one arm still around me. So there Hillary, I thought, you're not the only one.

Spencer wasn't much for awkward formalities.

"All right!" he cried, and quickly began to strip. Hillary and he were undressed and in the water before I realized what they were doing.

Benjamin and I stood alone.

"If you don't want to swim—" he began.

"It's a little windy."

"And your hair looks so pretty."

We stood, fully dressed, still hugging one another while Hillary's and Spencer's voices and laughter carried over the water, and the music from inside the club seemed to grow louder.

"Come on, Jen!" Hillary shouted.

"Come on!" Spencer shouted.

I looked at Benjamin. "Oh, hell," I said.

We turned our backs to each other modestly. As I fumbled with my zipper, my hands were shaking. I heard the clink of the brass buttons of Benjamin's jacket, his zipper, his shoes hitting the wooden planks. I took as long as I could, making meticulous pleats in my dress, and finally turned, shivering, to face him.

He hugged me again, more, I think, because he was embarrassed than because he wanted to hug me. He grinned and dove into the water, and I was standing by myself on the pier with my arms crossed over my breasts. I was cold, and I did not want to get colder. But now all three of them were calling for me to dive in, their heads bobbing like buoys, the lights fine and bright behind them, and I realized that the longer I stood there, the longer they would see me naked. I giggled and then dove into the warm dark water and surfaced in Benjamin's arms.

9

I woke the next morning at seven. I had forgotten Lulu, forgotten Daddy, forgotten Hillary and Spencer and why the sounds of their lovemaking had ever made me angry. My biggest concern was whether Benjamin would really appear at ten o'clock, as he'd said he would. I pulled on freshly laundered blue jeans and a T-shirt, not stopping to realize that Hillary had laundered them. It was only when I'd gone downstairs and found Lulu's garden empty again that I felt the blank gray pressure return. It would be the end of the summer. Three rabbits scampered like memories across the wet, lush lawn.

I left the family asleep and drove into town, singing along with the radio. I passed the cars lined up outside the Episcopal church and read the new Sunday inscription:

I LOVE THEM THAT LOVE ME: AND THOSE
THAT SEEK ME EARLY SHALL FIND ME

I drove on, and smiled at two boys riding their bicycles joyfully around a tree.

Main Street was almost deserted. Shadows from the linden trees dappled the pavement and the few cars. In the drugstore I bought a Sunday *Globe*, a pack of cigarettes and a small bottle of the perfume that Hillary wore.

I will be young again in lots of ways, but I will never be young again in precisely that way, and the proof was that I had never felt so old.

He was at the house at ten sharp. Only Hillary was awake, and I said good-bye to her through the bathroom door.

"When will you be back?" she called.

"What should I do?"

"When will you be back?"

"I don't know. Open up."

Instead she turned the water on. I pounded on the door.

"What?" she shouted, opening it.

She had no clothes on. Her tan lines created a pale, delicate bathing suit. She looked very thin. She was stunning and silver. I stepped into the bathroom and stood next to her before the mirror.

"Christ," I said. "I'm ugly."

"You're not ugly."

"Should I sleep with him?"

"Why not?" she asked, combing out her bangs.

"What if he doesn't want to sleep with me?"

"Then you won't have to decide."

10

Benjamin was silent on the drive to his house, which turned out to be just a quarter mile from Sithwell's Bay.

"Is something wrong?" I asked.

"I'm always quiet when I drive."

We stopped at the Sithwell's Bay store and bought fresh cream and fruit and coffee and flowers and the Sunday paper again. I found myself, like Lulu, suggesting he buy some juice because it was good for him.

His silence worried me. It never crossed my mind that he might be just as nervous as I.

The door to his house was painted bright red. A white Labrador retriever met us there. Benjamin made the introductions.

"Rufus, give the pretty lady your paw."

The house wasn't much bigger than Daddy's new studio. It had a polished wood floor, a huge stone fireplace, ragged red leather chairs, an antique enamel stove with a clock in it that worked. The house was built of new cedar and smelled like the inside of Lulu's stamp box.

I don't remember what we talked about as we scrambled the eggs and buttered the toast and ground up the coffee beans. I do remember that I was nervous and that I fussed over the table, finding a vase for the flowers, and wrinkled linen napkins in the back of a kitchen drawer, and Benjamin's mother's silver. I remember, too, that I washed the frying pan before I sat down to eat.

"Let it wait," Benjamin said.

"A good cook," I recited, "always cleans up after herself."

We ate and pretended to read the papers. At least I was pretending. I was remembering grimly the two freshman flings I'd had, how they had both started on drunken nights with back rubs. Benjamin and I were sober and there was daylight.

I began to clear the table, stacking the dishes in the kitchen sink, making lots of trips back and forth. Benjamin watched thoughtfully.

"Come here," he finally said, walking over to one of the big red leather chairs. I was spilling the juice he hadn't drunk down the drain. I turned off the faucet and looked at him. He grinned.

"Come here," he said again, and I went to stand next to him. He reached up, simple and straightforward, and drew me in, turning me around to sit between his legs. He rested his chin on my shoulder and held my breasts.

"Come here," he said for a third time, needlessly now. He bent my head forward, sweeping the hair from my neck so he could kiss me there. I believe that I shivered. His legs gripped mine. My back touched his chest. We leaned forward and back, waving like a reed. He stood me up and undressed me in the broad morning light. He undressed himself but I kept looking at his eyes.

"You're so beautiful," he said.

Benjamin, I thought. Benjamin and Jennifer. Hillary and Spencer. Lulu and Daddy.

"I want you," he said, "to teach me about love."

We made love on his bed. I lay beneath him and held tight. I stroked his back. I kissed his neck. I remembered what Hillary had told me once: "You can do anything at all in bed with a man except just *lie* there."

Benjamin talked to me, muttering words that were trite and obscene and oddly stirring. I did not answer or interrupt but once I groaned without meaning to. I felt something that deepened when we moved faster and stopped when we lay still. We drew lines with our fingers along each other's bodies, making patterns I wanted to see.

"Bennifer. Jenjamin," he said lazily.

"Us."

"What are you thinking of?" he asked.

"Oh, everything," I said.

"Everything?"

"And you?"

"Oh, nothing."

"That's not fair," I said.

"I know."

"Think of something."

"I'll think of you."

"I like the way that sounds."

"I thought you would."

We showered and dried each other off, and then he massaged me.

"You give a terrific back rub," I said.

"You have a terrific back."

We lazed and drifted through the afternoon, making love so many times that I gained a bit of confidence and once really looked at his body. He submitted to the inspection.

"So this is how it works," I said.

"That's about it."

"I guess I'm not as experienced as you."

"I like that," he said.

"You do?"

He nodded. "Classic male double standard. Count on it every time."

He stood up and walked over to the dresser and came back to bed with a wrapped present.

"Open it," he said shyly.

I was delighted.

"What is it?"

"Open it."

I did, thinking I would save the ribbon, save the box, save whatever was inside. It was a very old key, rusted, perhaps three inches long, with a square head.

"What is this?" I asked.

"This is the key to my heart."

"For someone who doesn't believe in love, you do a very good imitation."

"I watch a lot of old movies."

I laughed and hugged him, and we lay for a few minutes more, my head against his chest, his fingers combing my hair.

"I've got to go," I said.

"No you don't."

"Yes."

"Why?"

I faltered. "My folks," I said. "I've got to do something for them."

"Do they know you're here?"

"No."

"Why not?"

I shrugged.

"Don't tell me that Milo and Katherine Burke are prudish about these things."

"Of course not."

"Well, can I call you later?"

"Of course."

"Will you be there?"

"Of course," I said.

I saw the doubt in his face and a look of peevish displeasure that I almost couldn't believe.

"Benjamin," I said. "Where else would I be?"

11

But Benjamin didn't call that night, and he didn't call in the morning, and for the first time in my life I felt delicious anticipation turn gradually to disappointment, then anger and finally fear. He had to have meant it, I thought. He had to.

I should have guessed then that to be so thrown by one silence after one afternoon was a massive overreaction. But I thought it was only love. He had to have meant it. He gave me the key.

Daddy was in his studio, Hillary had gone for a run, and it was past lunchtime. I sat at the foot of Lulu's bed, watching her sip at the soup Hillary had made for her the night before. I had had to reheat it twice, as Lulu had fallen asleep each time she'd waited for it to cool. Now her cracked lips were stung by the salt in it, and I winced, watching her wince. She handed me the cup.

"You didn't eat the noodles or the vegetables," I said.

"I wasn't hungry."

"You've got to eat something, Lulu."

She smiled faintly.

"Light me a cig," she said.

I walked to her dresser and lit two of them at once, guiltily remembering how Benjamin had made me laugh the day before: after one particularly steamy session, he had lit six cigarettes at once, handing me three. I gave Lulu her cigarette, then checked her black book.

"Time for your pills," I said.

"I know."

"You get the prednisone this time."

"Oh goody."

"I thought you liked that one. Isn't that the up one?"

"I won't be able to sleep."

I handed the pills to her and poured a glass of water from the thermos on her night stand. Hillary had bought it in town a few days before. He had to have meant it, I thought. He said he was in love with me.

"Could you get some fresh water?" Lulu asked.

"This is fresh."

"It isn't cold."

"Sure it is."

"Jennifer."

He had to have meant it.

"If it's too much trouble—" she began, a phrase laced with sarcasm.

In the kitchen I cracked open an ice tray, making too much noise.

"What's wrong with you?" Lulu asked me when I handed her the glass. "Why are you sulking like that?"

"I'm not."

"What is it?"

"Benjamin said he'd call last night."

"Maybe he got tied up," she said.

"No."

"Maybe Harry needed him. Maybe he had to fly off-island."

"No."

She put her cigarette out, straining a little to reach the ashtray, only a foot or so away.

"How's your back?"

"All right," she said. "Now look. Maybe it's just as well, you know, Jen? You don't want to rush into anything." I slept with him yesterday, Lulu, I thought. Why hasn't he called. "You're too young to get too serious about just one boy," she said.

"You were my age when you met Daddy."

"Well, that's true."

"Mommy," I said, with all the drama the statement required. "Mommy, I'm in love with him."

And, oh, Lulu. Despite that—because of it—she did not laugh, did not so much as grin, did not say I was too young to know what love was. She simply took my hand in her own warm one, gave it a quick little squeeze and said, "He'll call, Jen, he'll call."

She told me to go for a walk. She said she'd leave a note on her door if he phoned while she was napping.

"A watched pot never boils," she said. That was another one.

I went down to the beach, walking along the rocks, picking up shells and beach glass. I recalled every word of his I could remember, every gesture I could still feel. I thought of ways to photograph him. I held the key he'd given me as if it were a rosary.

Without quite thinking about it, I wound up at the footbridge that led to Daddy's studio.

"Did you leave her alone?" he asked, without saying hello or looking up from the horse he was carving.

"Hillary's probably back by now."

"You left her alone?"

"Yes."

"Go back," he said.

I let the wind slam the door behind me. He had to have meant it.

Back at the house, there was no note on Lulu's door. I sat at the dining room table, drinking iced coffee and half reading the *Sentinel*. Hillary came in a few moments later, sweaty and out of breath.

"How is she?" she asked.

"Fine, I guess. I gave her the prednisone. She had some chicken soup. She's trying to sleep. She sent me away."

"She never sleeps after that one."

"Look, she *told* me to go for a walk."

"And you did? You left her alone?"

"Just for a few minutes."

"How could you be so stupid?"

"Oh, honestly."

She might as well have been performing her suicide scene as Juliet. "Never, *ever,* leave her alone again," she said.

"Yes, *Mom,*" I said, as she left the room to take a shower.

I lay on the porch in the sun, waiting and daydreaming. I needed him to call, needed our partnership confirmed, accepted. Us, I had said to him. Maybe that had frightened him. I wanted to be part of an us. I wanted time to have passed. I wanted to have known him longer than anyone. I wanted to be his best friend, and to have been his best friend, through good times I could imagine that afternoon and bad times I couldn't. I could see the afternoon, the day, the summer, from the sudden perspective of twenty years—the summer we met—and I loved the startling intensity, the sudden safety, of that perspective.

Hillary came outside in her bikini, carrying her Shakespeare and her suntan lotion.

"Want me to test you on your lines?" I asked.

"No. That's okay," she said.

"I'm sorry, Hills."

She began to work the tanning lotion into her arms.

"Are you still mad at me?" I asked.

"Not really."

"Then let's just skip this part, all right?"

She smiled, looking up to check the angle of the sun.

"Can we be normal now?" I asked.

"You're never normal."

"I slept with him."

"You're kidding." She spread her towel out next to mine.

"I'm not. I did. Yesterday. Four times."

"Four times," she said.

"Is that a lot?"

"Not bad for a beginner."

"I'm not sure I know what I'm doing yet."

"Trust me," she said. "You don't."

I reached into my pocket. "Hills," I said excitedly. "He gave me this key." I showed it to her. "He said it was the key to his heart."

She hooted, absolutely thrilled. "Oh, Jen," she said. "That's the oldest line in the book."

I sulked and pouted and lay in the sun until the heat became unbearable. Then I changed into a bathing suit and went down to the beach for a swim. Out in the cool water, floating on my back and looking at the sky, I decided that I would call him. He was the one, after all, who'd said he wanted to learn about love.

"Where is he, Harry?" I asked, after dialing the airport and getting through to the radio room. "Is he around?"

"Up in the air," Harry said gruffly.

"Oh."

"Left you there too?" He chuckled.

"Not at all," I said coolly. "What'd he tell you, Harry?"

"Nothing much. But I'd had a hunch, that's all. Turned out I was right."

I laughed, happy that Harry knew. If Benjamin had told him, I thought, then he had to have meant it.

"But Jennifer," Harry said, "give him room, you know? I'm telling you. I'm not going to say you called, you understand? I've seen more than one girl try to crowd my boy, and he's not that sort."

12

At seven o'clock, Hillary and I were sprawled at the foot of Lulu's bed. They were discussing strategies for me when the telephone rang.

"Be cool," Hillary hissed at me, handing me the phone. "No matter what he asks for, say no this time. You've got to make him wonder now."

I looked at Lulu. She nodded sagely.

"Hello, sweetheart," Benjamin said, and my eyes immediately filled with tears. Sweetheart. No one had ever called me sweetheart. "I've got to see you," he said. "Tonight. I'll drive by around nine, okay?"

"Okay," I said, and hung up.

Hillary and Lulu burst into laughter. I shrugged.

"So I'm not good at saying no," I said.

"What'd he say?" Lulu asked.

"He called me sweetheart. He's coming over at nine."

I left them laughing. I didn't care. I felt both grateful and giddy.

Benjamin took me down to the beach and we made love on the sand by the staircase. The stars were out over his head, and I could feel the smooth strong curves of the sand beneath me and his warmth and weight on top. We didn't make a sound for fear our voices would travel.

Then we sat against the staircase and wrapped a beach towel around us like a blanket.

"I've never felt this before," Benjamin said.

"Is that why you didn't call?"

"I guess."

"What was it?" I asked.

"I realized I couldn't take yesterday back."

"Do you want to?"

"I realized the only time you can lose something is when you have it."

"Do I have to tell you how backwards that is?"

"No," he said.

He kissed the top of my head. "We are seriously in need of cigarettes."

"Harry," I told him, "said I should give you room."

"Give me room? Like give me space? You mean like personal space? Like 'hey, man, I need some space' space?"

"That's the stuff."

"Old Harry."

"He said I shouldn't crowd you."

"All I want is to be crowded."

We stayed out there for a long time, saying little things I can't remember now.

13

It was during my lesson two days later, while we were doing the preflight, that I found what I'd been looking for.

"Ailerons?" Benjamin asked, standing by the plane as I moved the right wing's up and down.

"Check."

"Prop?"

I walked to the front of the plane and ran my hand over the cool blades.

"Check."

"Stop saying check."

"We don't *say* check," I said.

"That's right."

"Forgive me."

"You're forgiven."

We moved down to the empennage, and I tested the rudder and the elevator, moving one side to side, the other up and down. I noticed how simply they were connected, how regular, how much like normal hinges on a door. Nothing more complicated than a long wire pin was holding each hinge together.

Benjamin smiled at me. Planes buzzed in the air above us like painted dragonflies. If I took the pins out, the hinges would still look normal on the ground. The rudder and elevator would still move. Their pieces would still seem locked into each other. But in the air, with the force of the wind, they would not hold tight. Gradually they would shake loose from the tail, the flaps themselves might even fall, and there would be no way to steer.

I smiled back at Benjamin, who put his arm around me. In one way I had immediately ceased to need him, and I reveled in all the ways that were left.

It had been two weeks since our last lesson. I did not need to learn any more. So I let Benjamin fly us to New Bedford to pick up the book he had ordered for me. We walked past the spot where we'd had our picnic.

"Can you believe it's only been two weeks since you kissed me?" he asked.

"No," I said. "And *you* kissed *me*."

"Let's fly around today," he said. "I'll cancel my lessons. Let's go to Nantucket. Let's have a picnic."

"No," I said.

"Why not?"

"I have to get back."

His eyes got dark. "Why?"

"I just do."

"You've got a mysterious side," he said, but he was upset.

"Lulu says mystery keeps love alive."

"Is that one of my lessons?"

I laughed. "No," I said. "Let's go."
He frowned and reached for his keys.
"Is that the key to your heart?" I asked him.
"No," he said, sulking. "That's the key to my plane."

14

Hillary left two mornings later for her audition. I was not happy about her leaving—frightened, once again, at the prospect of being alone with Lulu, who had had two bad nights in a row. But Hillary said she'd be back the next day, and I had, after all, encouraged her to go. Then, too, her departure gave me an excuse to go to the airport without Benjamin's knowing I was there.

"Make sure she eats something," Hillary said as I walked her to the plane.

"I will."

"And do the dishes."

"I will."

"Give her ice for her lips if they're cracked."

"For God's sake. I know. Go," I said.

She walked toward the plane but stopped and turned back.

"I've got to get this part," she said.

"I know."

"For her."

"I know, Hills. Go."

I walked out to the tie-downs, avoiding Harry's office on the way. The grass was still dewy, and the field was deserted. I didn't see Benjamin. I didn't see anyone. I found Daddy's plane where it had been since our trip to the Cape. It seemed impossible that that had been only five weeks ago. Thinking of Lulu as she'd been for the last two nights, I wondered how a moment of faintness by the side of a road could have seemed so monumental. What Hillary and Daddy and I would give now, I thought, for a simple moment of faintness. Cancer reduces everything. Not just life and energy, dignity and hope. It reduces the size of the things you can be grateful for. They shrink from good weeks to good days to good hours. When you start to look for good moments, then you know what dying is.

I walked around to the back of Daddy's plane. I saw that the elevator on the tail was identical to Oscar's. The pins were even more visible because the paint had flaked off around the hinges. Daddy had been promising to give the Piper a new coat of paint for years.

I peered more closely at the elevator. I would need tools, but probably just a pair of pliers and a strong wire cutter. I didn't know how much time the whole job would take, but I realized that I could do it any night after we returned from the trip to Mass General on the twenty-sixth. I could even do it in stages, if need be. Nothing else that summer seemed to happen all at once.

I drove back to the house. The morning was still and clear. I wondered when I should tell Benjamin. I knew he would understand. I believed that if he knew what love was, he would know that it had no boundaries.

At home, I looked in on Lulu and was relieved to find her more chipper. She was not wearing her scarf. Her hair looked like a baby's, fine and fuzzy and close to her head. I told Daddy he could get back to work, and I settled at the foot of the bed.

"Milo," Lulu said girlishly, after he had left the room, "says he likes my hair like this. He says it looks cute."

"It does," I said, reaching for her book. The pain was a five. "You should have worn it short a long time ago," I said.

"He says he's going to sketch the beach next week."

"That's great."

"Rub my back?"

By the afternoon, she was feeling so much better that she decided to get up for a while. Leaning against me, her breathing rapid, she walked into the kitchen and sat on the hearth, her face ashen next to the red brick chimney. She wanted to give me a cooking lesson, she said, and she taught me how to make soup, laughing at my awkwardness, which I exaggerated for her benefit. But I wanted, suddenly, to learn from her all the things I had always begrudged her: how to run a household, cook, keep things in order, keep Daddy happy. I asked her how long it took to cook an artichoke and why you salted water to make it boil. I asked her how you used a fish knife and how you timed a meal so the meat and vegetables were ready at the same time.

These were tame questions, though their spirit was morbid—quick, tell me before you're gone—but Lulu was so amused at the thought of my sudden domesticity that she laughed along and teased me.

As the weeks passed, I asked her more questions, and more important ones. Had she been afraid of having children? Had it hurt? Had she ever been jealous of Daddy? Had she ever doubted his love? Had she ever not been in love with him? Had she ever had an affair? Had he?

I asked her every question I could imagine ever needing an answer to.

What would I ask her now? I would ask her why she gave

up her painting. How she put up with Daddy's distance. Why she lived so much through him and us. I would ask her if she knew her fears, and why she pretended she had none. I would ask her if she ever cried. I would ask her why she made her love contingent on conditions. Why she made us need her love so desperately, and if she knew that she had ours. Above all, I would ask her why she made me trust her answers so much more than my own.

15

Benjamin called that evening around six o'clock. It was Friday night, he said, and he wanted to celebrate with his girl.

"Am I really your girl?" I asked, as Lulu winked at me.

"You bet," he said.

"I can't see you tonight," I said.

Lulu gave me a warning look. I turned away from her.

Benjamin was silent. "Look," he finally said. "I love you. I want to see you. Just tell me. Should I be hurt or angry?"

"Neither," I said.

"What's this big secret of yours?"

"How about tomorrow?" I asked, trying, for Lulu's benefit, to sound casual. "Saturday. We can spend the whole day together."

"I'm more interested in the night."

"I can't talk now," I whispered tersely.

"I need a night with you," he said. "A whole night."

"So do I. With you."

"I want to wake up next to you. I want to watch you sleep."

"I'll call you tomorrow," I whispered.

"Tomorrow I may not care."

"Benjamin."

"I'm sorry," he said. "Tomorrow."

16

"My mother is dying," I said to Benjamin.

He stared at me, appalled.

"That's why I've had such a hard time seeing you. That's why I've had to be here. No one knows," I said. "Harry doesn't know."

We were walking down the beach. Benjamin had arrived at the house at nine o'clock, restless, defensive and braced for rejection. Daddy was at the house, within earshot of Lulu, sketching the beach. The last drawing, I thought. Now Benjamin was stunned and silent, and I was tragic and brave.

We found a dune that cut from the ocean to the lake. It was a sandy corridor, isolated, sunny, and he sat me down with my head against his chest and his legs around me. He began asking questions, first very technical questions about her illness—the prognosis, the medication, the doctors—then larger questions about our lives.

I told him about Daddy's work, his obsessiveness and

immersion, which I described as an attempt to please Lulu while escaping the truth about her. I told him about Hillary's pointless affair with Spencer, about her growing compulsiveness with the house, her growing similarity to Lulu—also escape routes, I said.

"And me?" he asked softly. "Am I your escape route?"

"No, Benjamin," I said. "God, no. You're real."

I told him about our winters in Boston and our summers on the island, about it'll all blow over and just because and you never know. I told him about her saying I was taking it well when I wasn't, and my telling her she was taking it well when she was. How she knew I wasn't a virgin, and how she hadn't laughed when I said I was in love. I told him about her gallery and The Boys, about her rabbits and Sam, about what she'd given up for Daddy and that I finally thought I understood why. I told him about her beauty and her humor and her sometimes unforgivable strength. I gave him her eulogy, sitting on the sand.

It was a pretty good speech and a true one, but it wasn't quite real. It was a speech meant to move him, and it did. It was meant to be part of some fantasy of need and concern that was as crucial to me then as it was a mystery. It was meant to make him love me, and it did that too, but of course what I failed to see was that he had loved me already. I failed to see that sympathy was only the smallest part of love.

We went for a swim. I flirted with him and teased, splashing water around him, diving down to grab at his ankles. He was relieved to have things between us normal, though of course they were not. Even Lulu, had she been eighteen, could not have added death to a first love affair and have everything come out normal.

But the morning itself was glorious. I can remember lying out in the sun after we swam, cool and tan, Benjamin beside me with one hand combing the sea grass and the other my hair. There was his hushed voice and his I love you, the warm sun-baked embrace and the exquisite sex.

17

Hillary came in at four o'clock. I met her at the airport.

"How's Lulu?" she asked.

"Sleeping."

"Daddy?"

"Doing his sketch. I don't know. Did you get it?"

"No."

"You didn't?"

"No."

Her voice was stuffy, her eyes still red.

"Oh, Hills," I said. "What happened?"

"It was between me and this kid. This *baby*. She goes to Harvard. She's got a *lisp*."

"Juliet was fourteen."

"Please, Jen. I've heard this fact once too often in the last twenty-four hours."

"I'm sorry."

She looked so dejected that I wanted to hug her. I touched her arm.

"Honest to God," she said, "this girl. She said 'Deny thy father and *refuthe* thy name.' "

"You'll get other parts," I said.

"That's what Lulu's going to say. God, I wanted to give this to her."

"But it's true, Hills. It'll be all right," I said. My turn to be Lulu.

We stopped at the car and sat on the front hood.

"I wanted this," she said softly. "I needed this very badly."

"Maybe you'll wind up with a better part because of it. You never know," I said.

She fiddled with the strap on her sandal.

"What am I going to tell her?"

"The truth."

"What am I going to tell her?"

18

But Lulu wasn't upset by the news. She was sad for Hillary, of course, but otherwise perfectly fine. I think Hillary's disappointment was actually a kind of gift to Lulu: in a way, it gave her the chance to be a mother again, to comfort Hillary, to be every bit herself.

They talked for hours. Daddy was still at his studio. The sun set, and the moon came out, and I decided to go find him.

It was strange on the beach, dark and windy. I could hear the waves, but I could not see them coming in.

Daddy wasn't working. He was sitting on the floor of his studio, paint cans and brushes all around him. Five horses stood in a circle. Only five of ten.

"I think I finally understand Lulu," I said.

"What do you mean?"

"What she gave up for you. Her painting. I never thought I'd understand."

"Don't give up your photographs."

"I won't," I said guiltily. "I won't."

He didn't say anything.

"Why aren't you working, Dad?"

"I'm tired."

"Come home, then."

"I will pretty soon."

"What is it, Dad?"

"It's obscene."

"What is?"

"To think of the world without her in it."

"Let me paint that rose," I said.

"All right. That red." He pointed to a can and a brush.

"She's going to love this, Daddy." I stood up and dipped the brush in the paint.

"That's not the point."

"Oh, Dad."

I started on the rose, very gently applying the paint, very careful not to drip.

"How can this happen? How can this happen?" he asked.

"What about God?"

"You know."

"What if everyone who knew someone died at the same time?"

"What?"

"All the people whose lives touched."

"Nothing is going to make this easy."

19

It is still embarrassing for me to recall the week that followed. I went absolutely wild with love. I held nothing back. Time, energy, heart, soul, mind—all given at once, like a bunch of sickly-sweet flowers. Benjamin has said since that the equation for that week was love $= x + 1$. Whatever x was, whether I was taking it or giving it, was not enough. Love, like Hillary and me in our childhood, was not allowed to stop growing, not allowed to reach any kind of plateau.

I sat in Daddy's studio while he carved the sixth horse, and I created an intricately drawn card for Benjamin that entitled the bearer to one free back rub. I drove into town and bought him aviator sunglasses and a tacky white pilot's scarf that I found in the island's thrift shop. We met on Main Street for lunch. Standing at the deli counter and surveying the signs—pastrami on rye; tuna on whole wheat—Benjamin began to giggle wildly.

"What?" I asked.

He couldn't talk.

"What? What?"

He pointed to a sign I'd missed: cream cheese on date.

"Excuse me," he managed to get out. "Could you put some cream cheese on my date, please?"

I started laughing too.

"Can't you just see it?" he asked between gasps. It was so silly. "A huge vat of cream cheese that you put your date under . . ."

We were attracting a lot of attention. We hobbled out onto the street.

"Cream cheese on date," he said.

"Cream cheese on date," I said. We giggled the way Hillary and I used to when we stayed up past our bedtime.

"Oh, you," he finally said, giving me a huge bear hug.

We drove to his house and made love. He drove me back to my house and we made love again—quietly, so no one would hear us. I gave him the sunglasses and the aviator scarf. He loved them. He gave me a water pistol. Later that evening he sat me down very seriously and told me that he had never been as happy in his life.

The next day I brought him half a cheesecake, saying he'd get the other half when he proved himself worthy. I wound up giving him the other half just an hour later. I wanted every day to be a photograph.

I gave him all the unlabeled keys that I could find around the house, each one wrapped in a separate box. I gave him twenty nesting boxes with a heart-shaped cookie in the smallest one. I knew that he loved me, and never believed it, and kept wanting to make him love me more. Climb this staircase, but before you rest at the landing, look—there's just one more stair.

Benjamin matched me step for step. He, too, was caught up, elated, convinced. He gave me flowers, poems, a computer printout of a thousand I love yous. He said I love you more often than he said my name. He said I had changed him. He gave me balloons, and thirty rolls of film to get me back to taking pictures, a better idea than either of us knew at the time and one I blithely ignored. I didn't want to be just me, taking pictures alone. I wanted to be us.

"You don't need to give me all these presents, you know," he finally said one evening.

"If you love someone," I said, "you want to give them things."

He let that go for the moment—along with a dozen similar sentences that began much the same way: if you love someone . . . if you're really in love . . . when someone really loves you . . . when you really know what love is. . . .

I cringe now, but I was on a sacred mission then. I was looking at Lulu and Daddy, delving into a past I didn't really understand while mimicking everything I thought I did. There was Daddy, carving this carousel. There was I, writing out quotations about love. I was showing Benjamin how to love, or so we both believed. What I was really showing him was the surface of a romance, and the emptiness that Lulu and Daddy had always filled for me.

20

But by Saturday, a week after I had told him about Lulu, Benjamin had had it. He was scared and depressed. He really did love me and really did share my sense of wonder. But he also suspected that love did not mean being welded together from the feet up. I had called him two or three times a day, not stopping to notice that I didn't give him a chance to call me, let alone to be by himself. If anyone had told me to draw back, even a little, I would have said it wasn't love.

I drove to Benjamin's house that day and gave him a large cardboard box with a number of objects in it, my latest creation.

"What is it?" he asked, not quite smiling.

"Open it."

Benjamin had told me that one of his favorite pastimes in the world was sitting in a tub with a crossword puzzle and a bowl of fresh peach ice cream. I had wrapped up a bowl, a spoon, a book of crossword puzzles, a bar of soap, a pen, a washcloth and a container of fresh peach ice cream that I'd convinced the parlor in town to make with the peaches I'd brought them. If there had been time, I probably would have grown the peaches myself.

But Benjamin did not take me in his arms when he unwrapped these gifts. He did not smile or say how lucky he was. He did not throw me on his bed and make love to me. He stared glumly at the floor and looked exhausted.

"What's wrong?" I asked him, honestly not knowing.

"Nothing much," he said.

"Don't you feel well?"

"Why do you keep giving me things?"

"I like to. I love you."

"Oh, sweetheart, I love you too."

I kissed his cheek.

"Do you want a back rub?" I asked.

"No. Not tonight."

I let it go. I went home and watched Hillary make dinner. I did not know what was happening. But when I called Benjamin late that night to say good night, he was monosyllabic and remote.

"Benjamin, what have I done?" I finally asked. "What's really wrong?"

There was a long pause.

"I'm not sure it's anything," he said. "It's probably just me."

"Why do you sound so strange?"

"I don't mean to," he said.

"Tell me what I've done wrong."

He forced a laugh. "No," he said. "I'm going to get some sleep."

"Do you want me to come there and sleep with you?" I whispered. "Is that it?"

"What about your mother?"

I had not wanted to spend nights away from the house.

"I could do it," I said.

"I don't think you should."

"I wish you would tell me what's wrong," I said.

"It's probably nothing that a good sleep won't fix," he said.

We hung up. It was an *it,* I thought. There was an *it* that needed fixing.

21

I had not thought much about Lulu that week. In part, of course, that was because of Benjamin. It was also because of Hillary, who seemed to have renewed her efforts since the audition to be nurse, cook and housemaid. But it was also because it would have been impossible to think about Lulu all the time. That is the myth about dying: that families freeze, that they never smile or argue while it's going on. I had done both all summer long, and I had also fallen in love. Lulu was always there, but there like the ocean's sounds in our house, sometimes clear and specific, more often not.

Sunday morning she returned, or rather I returned to her. I came downstairs to find Daddy and Hillary sitting together in the living room, hunched over coffee. They had both been up all night with her. The pain—the real pain—had returned, the way it had promised to that night before the party in July, and several times since. But this, they explained to me, had lasted for hours and hours.

"And now?" I asked.

"And now," Daddy said, "you sit with her, darling. Hillary gets some sleep, and I get back to work."

"Why didn't you wake me up?"

"Because we knew she'd need you today."

He took his coffee cup onto the deck, studying the landscape he had drawn so many times. I turned to Hillary.

"She likes it when you put the ice cubes in some gauze for her lips," she said.

I nodded.

"You'll have to take her to the john," she continued matter-of-factly. "She needs help sitting down and help getting up."

I waited a few moments after Hillary had gone upstairs, leafing through a book about Dürer. Then I went in to Lulu. I don't know exactly what I was expecting. I had kissed her good night, after all, just eight or ten hours before. And in fact little had changed. The shades were still drawn, and she was still on her right side, facing away from me, covered with the beautiful blanket she had crocheted.

"Jen?" she asked.

"That's right. It's me."

I got into bed with her, gently lowering myself behind her, beginning, once again, my slow massage. Her head, with its downy coat of hair, looked tiny resting on her arm. I noticed a horrible, hopeless, foreign smell, which is not a myth about death at all.

But I was spared, that morning anyway, from any true test of my mettle. Lulu seemed to have been exhausted by the night, and she had taken so many painkillers that she dozed in and out as I kept rubbing her back, saying nothing, watching the light trying to force its way in through the venetian blinds. When Hillary came back four hours later, my body was stiff and my hands were numb, but I looked up at her guiltily. It seemed she had been through the worst.

We stood together for a few moments, looking down at our mother, who was rapidly ceasing to be our mother, becoming, instead, some kind of child.

"I guess we can leave her to sleep," Hillary whispered. "She'll call us if she needs us."

"Girls," Lulu said. She half sat up in bed. She looked scared. Hillary knew immediately and rushed to Lulu's side, picking up a small bucket from her night table that I hadn't noticed. Hillary held Lulu's head as she vomited, gasping from the strain it put on her back. I stared at the two of them, staying as long as I could, and then ran from the room.

The beach was sunny and incongruous. My face was hot and I felt sick and trapped. I ran, tripping over the rocks. The damned rocks, I thought. I hated Hillary for giving what I couldn't give, and Lulu for needing it. I pounded on Daddy's studio door. He let me in, a paintbrush in his hand.

"What's happened?" he asked, seeing my face.

"Lulu got sick," I said. "Hillary's with her." I burst into tears. "I couldn't take it, Daddy." He embraced me. "I couldn't take it." He dropped his paintbrush behind me, hugging me hard. I cried, remembered my vow to be strong, and cried harder.

"Jen," he whispered. "Don't be so tough on yourself. She loves you. You know that. She knows you love her. That's what counts."

"I wish," I finally managed to say, "that I could just give her more."

"I know."

"*You* can give her the carousel."

He broke our embrace, standing back from me warily. I looked around the room, counting the horses.

"Six," I said. "You've only done six."

"That's right."

"You've got four more to do! What are you *doing* here?"

"Now listen to me," he said, putting his arm around me and walking me to the door. "I'm talking as a sculptor now and not as your father."

"What."

"I want you to go home and help Hillary. And I don't want you to come back here until I tell you that you can."

"But, Daddy."

"Listen to me, Jen. I need to work alone."

"But she's never going to see it!"

"She doesn't have to see it."

"How can you *say* that?"

"Go now," he said gently. "Please, darling. I've got things on my mind."

I couldn't understand. All I knew was that I could not help Daddy give the carousel, or Hillary give the physical comfort. But I could give Benjamin, I thought. I could show Lulu that she'd taught me how to love.

I called him when I got back to the house and told him the whole day's story, completely forgetting his distance from the night before. I refused to acknowledge the foreign tone that crept back into his voice. I asked him if he'd fly Lulu and me to Boston on Saturday. I wanted Daddy to keep working, and Lulu and Hillary to know that I wasn't scared. Reluctantly, Benjamin agreed.

"Are we going to have a lesson Wednesday?" I asked.

"I thought you didn't want lessons any more."

I waited. "I thought you did," I said.

"What do you mean?"

"About love. Remember what you said?"

Benjamin sighed.

"I'll call you," he said.

"I don't really want a flying lesson," I said.

"I know."

"But maybe I could bring you lunch."

"Call first."

"Cream cheese on date?" I asked.

He laughed faintly.

"I'll see you Saturday," he said.

I couldn't believe that was all he'd say, but something told me not to push it. I didn't bring him lunch on Wednesday. I worked, instead, on a birthday photograph for Lulu. I took two old ones from years before and mounted them, facing each other, just like a queen of hearts. I drew a flower in each hand. I drew crowns and costumes and a heart in each corner.

Stroking her back late that night, I said:

"What Daddy's working on. It'll make you very happy."

"I don't want to hear about it," she said.

"You don't?"

"He'll tell me when he wants to."

I didn't call Benjamin until Friday night, and then only to make plans. We'd fix it all tomorrow, I thought. I'd smile at him. He'd meet Lulu, and then he'd understand. He agreed to have the plane ready by eight o'clock the next morning. There was barely any warmth in his voice at all. I told him I'd give him a wake-up call, and he thanked me and said good night. I'd fix it in the morning, I thought.

22

I woke at seven and called Benjamin. There was no more love in his voice than there had been the night before. But he offered to pick us up at the house. I told him we'd meet him at the airport, and then I went back to bed. I lay there, looking out the window, feeling myself panic: everyone seemed to be leaving me at once.

It had rained the night before. Dozens of small insects had been trapped in the screen. It was time for new screens, I thought. My eyes filled with tears. When I was very little and afraid of the dark, Lulu had come up to my bedroom one night when she heard me crying. She had sat on my bed with me and made me look at the window. She had told me that if I was really scared then she would take the screen down from the window and needlepoint on it the exact view beyond it of the ocean, the trees and the sun. Then, she had told me, she would put the screen back, so it could always be daytime for me, until I wanted the night.

Hillary pounded on the door.

"Everyone's up," she said. "Get moving."

It was a gray day, and I worried that it would rain.

"I'm sure it'll all blow over," Lulu said. But it took Hillary and me almost an hour to dress her. She was stiff and swollen and exhausted by the smallest exertions. Hillary had gone to town the day before to buy the dress for Lulu. It was a large loose cotton shift that would not be tight around her swollen stomach. It was the kind of dress, sleeveless and crepey, that fat women wore. I hated the way she looked in it, and I hated Daddy's seeing her that way because I was sure that she did. But she tied a bright scarf around her head and put on a lot of jewelry and didn't look in the mirror.

"You're sure you don't want me to take you?" Daddy asked.

"I want you to work."

"But this boy," Daddy said.

"He's not a boy," I told him.

"Anyway," Lulu said, "he's probably a better pilot than you are."

Daddy hesitated. "At least I'm going to drive you two to the airport," he said. "Jennifer doesn't look awake yet."

I was sleepy. I sat in the back seat alone. Lulu and Daddy were lighted from the sun up the road. They became silhouettes again

Benjamin was waiting for us by his plane.

"Mr. Burke, Mrs. Burke. It's a pleasure," he said.

He and Daddy shook hands.

"I'd like you to take my plane," Daddy said.

"Of course."

"My daughter trusts you," Daddy said.

"She has every reason to, sir."

"It's my family."

"I realize that, sir," he said.

Lulu stretched out her left hand. Her right was linked in Daddy's arm.

"Benjamin, it's a pleasure," she said. "I'm glad you use your full name. I don't think Ben is as nice."

We walked around to Daddy's plane, and Benjamin eased Lulu away from Daddy, helping her up into the seat. He was every bit the gentleman, and he hadn't looked at me once.

23

We drove up to Mass General in a rented car at around one o'clock. A nurse was there to help Lulu. Benjamin waited until they were inside.

"I'll see you in a few hours," he said.

"You're not going to wait with me?"

"No."

"Why not?" If you loved me, I thought, you'd want to wait with me.

"Lulu would be uncomfortable with me there. She may need you."

"That's not true."

"I don't want to argue," he said. "Anyway, she's waiting for you."

"Do you hate me?" I asked.

"Of course I don't hate you," he said, sounding disgusted. "I'll see you in a few hours."

Inside, Lulu was waiting by the front desk. There was a tight sick smile on her face. Walking down the corridor to

Dr. Irving's office, she gripped my hand and I squeezed back. Her hand was hot and sweaty. It had been a long time since we had held hands, and hers had seemed much larger then. "Take Mommy's hand," I remember her saying when we walked down a crowded street. "Hold tight."

"Are you scared?" I asked.

"Don't be ridiculous."

But *I* was.

The nurse in Dr. Irving's waiting room said that Lulu should undress. So I went with her into a small examining room and helped her into a hospital gown. She had to put on those ridiculous plastic elf shoes, which made us both laugh. But she was stiff with pain, stiffer even than she had been that morning.

We went back out to the waiting room. There was no one there except a tall redheaded nurse who frowned when Lulu lit a cigarette.

"Where's Benjamin?" Lulu asked.

"I don't know. I think he's mad at me."

"Why?"

"I don't know."

"You've been too available."

"But I love him," I said. "Why do I have to play games?"

"Don't talk any more," she said.

"Are you nervous?"

"Hush," she said.

"Do you feel sick?"

"Hush!"

I waited a few moments, thinking, all right, so she doesn't want me to treat her as though she's dying. She wants to be treated like Lulu.

"With Benjamin," I said again softly, "why do I have to play games?"

"Don't *talk* any more," she snapped.

"But you *asked.*" It came out fast and angry, like a little girl's whine.

Lulu smoothed her bandanna with her left hand and looked away from me. I felt like standing up and taking her by the shoulders and shaking her hard. I felt like screaming at her, What right do you have? What have I done wrong? How can you do this? Where is my mother? I sat listening to the rain hitting the air conditioner outside the window. The blinds were drawn tight. Next to the receptionist's desk, three wheelchairs were lined up like spectator seats. If Lulu had been the daughter, I thought, she would have known what to say, and when. If Hillary were here, I thought, she wouldn't be angry.

"Well, Katherine," Dr. Irving said when he walked in. He must have been horrified by the change in her, but he didn't show it, except to run a nervous hand through his bushy white hair. Lulu winked at me. She always said that Dr. Irving was as proud of his white hair as he was of his medical degrees. She met him with a cool, even look. Instantly he grinned.

"Same old Katherine," he said. "You still hate doctors, don't you?"

"I hate being sick."

"Same old Katherine."

He checked her pulse against a heavy Rolex watch.

"Where's that husband of yours?" he asked.

"I made him stay behind and work."

He laughed, fixing his hair again with one hand, and with the other motioning to the receptionist to bring over one of the wheelchairs.

"Not on your life," Lulu said. "I'll walk." Her shoulders went back just perceptibly. "And where's there a phone that Jennifer can use?"

"This is Jennifer? I thought it was Hillary."

"Hi," I said. "I'll come with you, Lulu," I said, trying my hardest to sound like her.

"No," she said, and I knew I had failed to convince her. "You call Milo. Tell him we're fine. Tell Hills to make something good for dinner. This won't take long." She arched an imperious eyebrow at Dr. Irving. "Will it, Jonas?" she said more than asked.

"No, ma'am," he answered. "Not if you say so."

He offered his arm to her with his elbow hooked, as if he were leading her onto a dance floor.

I called home five or six times while Lulu was getting her treatment, but there was never any answer. I could imagine Daddy in his studio, head bent low over one of his horses while the phone rang in the empty house. I could imagine Hillary, strong long legs running the dirt road in the rain. As the afternoon wore on and I had leafed through every outdated magazine in the waiting room, I began to imagine Benjamin too. Maybe he had gone off to get some fabulous picnic dinner for the ride home. Maybe he had invented some wonderful surprise. I tried to think what I would do in his place: go to Quincy Market, perhaps, and buy a puppet or a pound of cookies.

I went downstairs to make sure Benjamin was there with the car before Lulu came down. He pulled up and gave me a faint smile.

There was no surprise.

"How is she?" he asked.

"Not good," I said.

But when I brought her downstairs ten minutes later, she seemed perfectly fine. Perhaps the nearness of the hospital and the future had shocked her. Perhaps it was Jonas Irving, whom she wanted so much more to laugh at than to need. Perhaps it was the relief of having the treatment over. Perhaps she knew it would be her last fully conscious day.

"Turn off here," she told Benjamin as we drove down Route 125.

"It's the next exit, I think," he said.

"No. I want to check in on The Boys."

So we did. We let her off on Boylston Street, and by the time we had parked the car and caught up with her, she had already gone on to visit some friends in a nearby shop. She was trying to stop dying again, but for once I couldn't let her. She was dying and I was going to believe it, no matter how sure her steps suddenly seemed, no matter how convincing her smile. She was dying and she tried to rob me of that knowledge with every gallery she needed to see, every artist she said hello to on the street, every bit of pride and energy she somehow summoned. She tried to take it back that afternoon, take her life back, and I couldn't let her. I had something to say to Benjamin about the preciousness of time that her buoyancy seemed to contradict. And I had been up and down with her too many times by then. I watched her bitterly, knowing that worse would come.

But somehow she held on. We took off with cloudy skies and had to stop on the Cape. The tower at Fall River was reporting thunderstorms. Benjamin left us sitting in the plane and went into the terminal to check the weather. He returned after a few minutes to say we would have to spend the night. There was a solid bank of storms on the way.

Lulu fell asleep as we waited for Benjamin to find a car. I reached in front to cover her with a blanket. It was almost completely black out the window. Benjamin had cut the power in the plane, so the cockpit was dark too. I watched the water as it ran down the windows and ran off the wings. The skylight above me was a tightly stretched drum, with the raindrops hitting it. It made me think of Daddy's studio and its funny black canvas roof. At intervals a beacon from the tower lit the wing and Lulu's face.

"I love you," I whispered to her.

24

All Benjamin could get was a van, so we put Lulu in the back seat. The rain was so heavy that he had to pull over every now and then because he couldn't see the road at all. I was very scared. I wanted to know, or say, that it would all blow over. Benjamin's shoulders were hunched forward as he looked for the road.

We finally saw a sign that said inn. It actually only said "NN," but when I pointed that out to Benjamin he didn't even smile. I felt the panic I'd felt that morning.

We followed the signs through wet, curving roads and stopped at a long wide gate with the words MILLERTON INN painted in white on graying wood. Benjamin got out to open the gate. The inn was a long, low shingled house, and behind it were a barn and a silo. Water coursed through the drainpipe near us, and in one place, where the pipe was missing, just streamed off the roof like a waterfall.

"I'm hungry," Lulu said, waking up. She hadn't been hungry for days. It was as if all the miles we had traveled that day had been time going backward, and the damage and the wretched nights were being undone.

"We've got two rooms," Benjamin said when he came back with an umbrella. "That's all they have."

He helped Lulu up the front steps, carrying the umbrella for her. I scampered behind in the rain. Several dozen moths that had been resting on the door flew off with the shadow from her hand. She laughed.

We walked into the lobby. A bald man with a white mustache was standing behind the desk. Patchwork quilts were hung on high walls all around us and up the staircase. Candles were lit everywhere, and there was a fire in the fireplace. Two tall rockers stood on each side of it, empty, like the ones in Lulu and Daddy's room.

"You're lucky," the man said. "We're full up. A couple of folks never showed this weekend. Must have been the storm."

Lulu walked over to the fireplace.

"You don't look all that busy," Benjamin said.

"Full up."

"How many rooms have you got here?" Benjamin asked.

"Three."

They laughed together. I looked over at Lulu while Benjamin signed us in. She was examining the portraits that were hanging over the fireplace. There were two of them: one a man, one a woman. Their clothes were mostly black, their faces so pale they looked almost blank except for faint dots of color in their cheeks. Their eyes were full and deep.

"Phillips," Lulu said. "Ammi Phillips. Around 1820." She turned back to us, satisfied.

"Is there anything to eat?" Benjamin asked the man.

"Sure, sure," he said. "I've got just the thing for you folks. Fresh clam chowder. Rose made it this afternoon. Just follow me in. We'll heat it up. Then you can go upstairs."

Lulu stayed at the desk to call Daddy. The man led the

way through a tangle of L-shaped corridors. The whole house seemed to be listing slightly to one side. The barn-red floorboards creaked as we walked.

The dining room table was made up of four wrought-iron squares put together to form a larger square. In the center were eight earthenware jugs filled with hyacinths and daisies. Around them was a circle of twenty-one candles, each in a long, graceful pewter candlestick holder.

"You'll want to know why twenty-one," our host said, long before we would have counted. "Well, I married Rose on the twenty-first of March."

Around the room's periphery—on side tables and shelves and mantels—were still more candles, some in green glass bottles, some in silver, some in hurricane lamps, some in old mustard jars. The walls had been painted, long ago it seemed, with scenes of whaling expeditions. There were more old portraits above the doors to the kitchen. I had never seen a room as haunted or as beautiful.

Lulu joined us. She had finally begun to fade. I saw her reach in her purse for some pills when she sat down. Across the candlelit table, I tried to meet Benjamin's eyes, but he wasn't looking for me. I couldn't eat, and Lulu had lost her appetite too.

After dinner, Benjamin and I went upstairs to check on the rooms. They were next door to each other, both large and slanted and wooden, both with a large four-poster bed. I grinned at Benjamin.

"You'd better take this one," he said. "It's bigger."

"What?"

"This one's bigger."

"Where are you going to sleep?"

"In here," he said, pointing to the smaller room.

I had had it. I waited as long as I could before I spoke, but I was still crying.

"Oh, Benjamin," I said.

"Don't cry," he said. "I just thought it would be awkward with your mother, that's all. I thought she wouldn't want us to be sleeping together."

"It doesn't matter," I mumbled.

"I was only trying to think of her."

"Two weeks ago you wouldn't have cared. Two weeks ago you'd have made me sleep with you, no matter what."

He stared at the floor, speechless. I looked at him, imploring.

"I don't care what you say tomorrow," I said, desperate. "I don't know what's on your mind and you obviously won't tell me. But I need you tonight. Please don't be mean to me. Please don't."

He softened. "All right, sweetheart," he said. "I'm sorry. I really am. I'm sorry."

"It's just too much," I said. "I can't lose it all at once."

Later, as we lay in bed, his body curled around me like a hand, and I thought it would be all right.

25

We were home by ten the next morning. The flight was calm. Hillary met us at the airport and drove us home. I didn't even wait to see Lulu tucked in. I went straight to the garage and took the biggest pair of pliers I could find. I got into the car and drove off without saying good-bye. I went to the hardware store, where I bought a pair of heavy wire cutters. On my way to the airport, I didn't bother to pass the church.

I parked in the airport lot and left the tools under a map in the glove compartment. I found Harry in the radio room.

"He's out on the field," Harry said when he saw me. "Got a lesson in a few minutes."

I thanked him and walked out the back door. I could see Benjamin in the distance, leaning against Oscar, the yellow rag in his back pocket as always. He was talking and laughing with some pilots. He was easy, relaxed. He ran a hand through his hair. He cocked his head to one side, listening. I smiled as I approached him. I watched him say something to his friends and watched them scatter like rabbits. The smile had faded from his face. I had taken it away from him.

I walked directly into his arms, which were limp and foreign.

"Come with me," he said, as he had just a month before. As we had then, we walked to the split-rail fence and sat side by side on top of it.

"I don't think," he said, holding my hand, "that this is going to work right now."

"I know that's what you think," I said. "I also know you're wrong."

He sighed.

"Do you love me, Benjamin?"

I watched, amazed and relieved, as his eyes filled with tears.

"Yes," he said. "Yes. Of course I love you. I'm also not sure that we agree on what that means."

A plane took off in front of us, and I waited for the noise to fade.

"If you love someone," I said, "you become a part of them. You can't go away. You're family. You have them inside you. If you argue it's like having a fight with yourself."

"That's your family," he said.

"That's right."

"Look what they do to you! Do you realize what they do to you? Christ. Don't you ever get a break?"

"My mother is *dying*," I said. "What do you expect?"

He sighed again. "It's more than that," he said softly. "You just can't see it."

"I see two people who are in love."

"You can't *know* that," he said.

"Of course I can."

"No."

"Just because yours weren't happy—"

"That's not it."

"Fine."

He let a few moments pass. "Even if your parents were as perfect as you think—"

"I didn't say they were perfect."

"Even if they were."

"What."

"You're not Lulu. I'm not your father."

He stared at me. Don't let go of my hand, I thought.

"Couldn't we make up our own definitions?" he asked.

"You wanted me to teach you about love."

"You ask too much of me."

"But you get so much from me."

"I have to think," he said. "I can't think."

He let go of my hand. I stared at it, then him. He wiped a tear from his cheek. Just one tear, I thought.

"Couldn't we just tone this down a bit?" he asked.

"I'm not going to be your friend."

"Isn't there anything in between?"

"No."

"I have to give a lesson now."

He walked back to his plane.

After he had taken off, I went to the car and got the tools. Back at Daddy's plane, I felt very calm. No one seemed to notice me. It took only about twenty minutes to remove four of the pins. I tested the flaps gently. Daddy would never be able to tell.

26

The day in Boston had, in fact, been Lulu's last real day, the last day she was conscious for more than a few hours at a stretch. It could have been the day's exertion that made her start her slide, but no one has ever blamed me for not stopping her. In part that's because they knew I couldn't have, no matter how hard I might have tried. In part, too, it was because while we were at the inn, Dr. Irving had called Daddy to say he'd have a bed waiting for her at Mass General. It had gotten that bad. Lulu's forty-ninth birthday was just a few days away.

We did not know if she would live that long, or if she would live fifty days or five hundred. No one seemed to be able to say. We didn't even know what we were waiting or looking for. Daddy tried to explain to me what Dr. Irving had said: the radiation would either lead her into remission or it would not. If it didn't, he said, we would certainly know.

In the meantime, we prepared ourselves for Lulu's birthday. Daddy asked her what she wanted most.

"I want a pack of peppermint Life Savers," she said.

"Is that all?"

"But I want you to pick it out very carefully."

It was Monday afternoon. Benjamin had not called. I was beginning to believe that he wouldn't.

I walked down to the beach. He hadn't really loved me, I thought. Real love would have been like real pain: private, persistent, inescapable. I thought of Daddy's carousel. I thought of the plane. It would be the end of the summer. I would lean into the cabin to say good-bye. My heart quickened. I stopped walking. It *was* the end of the summer. The island was emptying out. The plane was ready now, and I thought I was too. Of all the changes the summer had brought, this was the one thing that hadn't been altered, the one thing I would give. Even Benjamin, I thought proudly, hadn't been able to change this for me.

I looked out at the waves, imagining that what I was doing was freezing them in mid-crash, before they broke and splintered.

Daddy joined me on the beach.

"I want you to drive into town," he said. He reached into his back pocket and brought out his wallet. His fingers were covered with dried paint of every color. He handed me seven twenty-dollar bills. "I want you to buy every dictionary you can find," he instructed me. "It doesn't matter what the languages are. Buy a thesaurus too, or a synonym dictionary. Definitions."

"Why?"

"Lulu's birthday present."

"What present?"

"Her birthday present," he said again.

"What about the carousel?" I asked.

"Come on," he said. "Get moving."

"But Daddy."

"I've *told* you, Jennifer. Hurry. We'll talk later. And one other thing," he said as I started to go.

"Right," I said. "I know."

"Peppermint Life Savers," he said with a smile.

I drove to town and bought the books, thirteen of them in all. I made four or five trips to the car. A few of my books had sold, I noticed. I wondered who had actually bought them. Maybe, I thought, they'd just been put away. It didn't matter at all.

There was no message from Benjamin when I got home, only Lulu and Hillary together, quiet.

"How is she?" I whispered, walking into the bedroom.

"Ten," Hillary whispered back.

27

Legend has it that on August 29 in 1777, Sanders Island made a singular contribution to the Revolutionary War. On that day, the island's residents banded together to hide their livestock from the approaching British. Every last cow, horse, pig, chicken and goat was stashed from view. The fact that the British never came changed nothing. Every year since then, the island's selectmen had voted for fireworks and a parade that made the Fourth of July seem pale by comparison.

I had looked forward to this night, had imagined spending it with the family and Benjamin. We had even talked about it. Now it was impossible.

Hillary made lobster bisque, salad and fresh bread. Lulu ate almost nothing and was very quiet. She only sat up with us for half an hour or so, and then we took her back to bed.

After dinner, we did what we had always done: moved the couches out from the living room wall and turned them to face the water. The room was dark as we waited for the sun to set and the stars to come out, and then I watched as the lights opened up onto the water. I knew from too many past summers that I shouldn't even try to take pictures, so I didn't. I just watched. Daddy sat, restless, alone, and carved a small block of wood away to nothing. Hillary cleaned up the shavings and brought him a Scotch, and I sat by myself on the ottoman, thinking of Benjamin.

We sipped our drinks. I thought of other nights like this one, and how our house had seemed so festive, and how the Scotch had made me drunk. Now I drank and felt nothing. There were only the three of us and the sounds of the boats in the harbor honking their horns at each display. Later, when I tried to sleep, I could hear laughter from the people on those boats, and Daddy's footsteps as he paced on the deck below us.

28

Daddy had taken a block of his best oak. Out of it he had carved a box, making wooden hinges for its top. He had sanded and polished the inside surface until it felt like the inside of a shell. On the top and sides, Daddy had used the dictionaries I had brought him. He had cut out every definition of the words love, lover, loving, lovable, love affair, love bird, love child, love knot, lovelorn, loving cup, lovely. All our dictionaries still have a missing page.

Daddy had made a collage of these definitions, arranging them meticulously, coating them with so many layers of shellac that reading the words was like reading through glass. In places, too, he worked in some colorful drawings—cherries, strawberries, daisies, rabbits, a sun and a moon with ink-drawn lines of light. The package of Life Savers fit with room to spare.

I had wrapped my queen of hearts in old copies of the *Sentinel*, drawing a ribbon on the package with a red marker. Hillary's present was a large white lace nightgown, sleeveless, cotton, with ample room. Typically, it made the most sense of all our gifts. It was a gift given to Lulu now, not Lulu in the past or future.

We waited through a foggy, hot afternoon, watching the sun move across the sky. Daddy did not even try to work.

At around three o'clock, Hillary went to the kitchen and emerged an hour later with a delicious potato leek soup that no one could eat. Daddy excused himself from the table. We could hear the hiss of the screen door closing behind him, and his caged footsteps up and down the deck.

"I can't stand this," Hillary said quietly.

"I know."

"Why doesn't he *talk* to us?"

"I know."

"I wish I believed in something."

"That's just what he said the other day."

She cleared the dishes.

"What would *she* be doing, Hills? For him?"

"She'd be telling him that everything's going to be all right."

"It'll all blow over."

"But it won't." She looked truly upset. She began to wash the dishes, painstakingly scrubbing every last pot and pan. She had become the guardian of that particular Lulu flame, the keeper of the kitchen.

"Have you said anything to her about it?" she asked.

"Like what?"

"I don't know. Just about it, I guess. You're the one who's always having the talks. Does she know?"

"She must," I said.

"But you haven't asked her?"

"I just keep telling her I love her," I said.

"Me too. It's all I can think of saying."

29

It wasn't until midnight that Lulu was awake enough to have her birthday. Hillary brought in a brownie she had baked after she cleaned up the kitchen. It had a single candle in it.

"Make a wish," Hillary said, looking sick.

Lulu closed her eyes, brought her cracked lips together and blew out the candle.

"I wished—" she began foggily.

"Don't tell us."

"I wished that I would marry a sculptor," she said, "and have two lovely girls."

Hillary backed out of the room slowly. Lulu did not see her go.

Daddy and I unwrapped her presents for her, but she was drugged and in pain, and she felt more than saw them. I left her alone with Daddy.

Upstairs, I heard running water in the bathroom. I opened the door. Hillary was sitting in the bathtub, naked and crying. She had her legs crossed, and she was holding on to her ankles. She hadn't put the stopper in the drain. The water streamed down, splashing over her hands and feet and running out. Hillary was red-faced and hysterical and skinny. I could see the outline of her ribs every time she tried to catch her breath.

"Hillary," I said.

"Oh, Jen."

She reached up like an infant for me with two wet arms. I knelt down by the tub and she knelt up inside it and we hugged each other very hard. She kept crying.

"I didn't believe it," she finally managed to say, her words dull and stuffy above the running water.

"It's all right, Hills," I said. "It's going to be all right."

SEPTEMBER

1

I took over from Hillary the next day. I sent her to town to buy groceries, and she went, relieved to be going. She was numb and exhausted, and she was Hillary again, not this manic imitation of Lulu. Even she could not keep playing the role.

I cleaned the kitchen and made coffee. I remembered the summer's first morning, when Lulu had made Daddy that second pot. I brought a cup into the bedroom for him. Lulu was asleep. Daddy emerged from the bathroom as I came in. He looked old. I hugged him.

"You going to work?" I whispered.

"I don't want to leave her just yet," he said.

"Stay then."

"Maybe I will."

He stretched out on his side of their bed, looking at her with the same dull disbelief I'd seen the night before. I went into the bathroom and cleaned the sink and folded the towels Daddy had used. When I came out again, they were holding hands. It didn't hurt. They were almost gone, and I knew they would go together. Lulu was speaking to him softly from her drugged, almost painless world. He was leaning close to hear her better.

"Hey, kid," she was saying. "Remember? Remember Sithwell's Bay? Remember those martinis on the dock?"

Daddy stared at her, then gently disengaged himself.

"Of course, kid," he said, his voice shaking. "Remember?"

He bolted from the room.

Quickly I lay down in his place and took her hand.

"Remember?" she asked again.

"Sure I do, Lulu," I said.

"Where'd Daddy go?"

I forced a laugh. "Maybe to get some martinis," I said. She smiled, closed her eyes and went back to sleep.

I left the bedroom quietly. Out on the deck, Daddy was standing at the railing, looking down at the beach. His hands clutched the peeling white wood. His shoulders shook. I'd never seen him cry before. It horrified me. It made me sure. He cried just as Hillary had the night before—huge, uncontrollable, infant tears. I put my arms around him, dry-eyed, just as I'd been with Hillary.

I've got it all fixed, I wanted to say. I felt the sun on my face.

"Did you see how she smiled?" he asked me, sobbing.

"Yes, Daddy."

"How can she *be* like this? How can she smile?"

"I don't know."

"It's not *fair.*"

"Why don't you go to work?" I asked.

"I'm staying with her today."

2

Late the next afternoon, I was stretched across the foot of Lulu's bed, staring at the ceiling, sharing a cigarette with her. She was saying that I should cut my hair. I was marveling at her stamina. Haircuts. Cancer. Dying is not the same as death. The phone rang. I met Lulu's eyes.

"Let it be him," I said, jumping up to answer it, handing Lulu the cigarette. She puffed at it meditatively as I said hello. It was Benjamin.

"Is it?" Lulu whispered.

I nodded.

"Do what I tell you," she said, reaching for her black book and pen.

"How's your mother?" Benjamin was asking.

"All right," I said cautiously. "How are you?"

"Fine." There was a silence. I looked at Lulu helplessly as she started to write in the book.

"What have you been up to?" I asked him, stalling. I

leaned toward Lulu, stretching the phone cord as far as it could go, trying to see what she was writing.

"Well," Benjamin said, "I've been irascible, tired and headachy. Today I disconnected the Muzak speaker in the office. I just couldn't stand it. But I thought Harry was going to kill me."

"That's too bad," I said, while Lulu held out the book for me to see. Next to her most recent entry—"2 painkillers, pain 5, ate a piece of toast"—she had written "Sound more cheerful" and three exclamation points.

"But you know what?" I continued, not breaking stride, sounding infinitely more cheerful. "I've really missed you!"

Lulu shook her head violently, waving her arms. I started to smile.

"All wrong!" she wrote. "Too busy to miss him."

"But I've been really busy too," I said. At this Lulu started to laugh quietly. I tried to keep a straight face and to keep the laughter out of my voice. There was a long, un-funny silence coming across the wire, but I suddenly didn't much care.

"So what else is new?" I asked, still grinning at Lulu.

"I really just wanted to hear your voice."

"Oh?" I said, grabbing the pen from Lulu and writing "Wanted to hear my voice."

"Sing something?" she wrote back.

"That's right," Benjamin said warmly. "I missed hearing your voice."

"Want me to sing something?" I asked, giving Lulu the okay sign.

Benjamin laughed. "No," he said awkwardly. "I'll be in touch, sweetheart."

I hung up and laughed giddily with Lulu, reporting every word he'd said, the inflections in his voice. Benjamin would either have it or he wouldn't, would either become one of us or he wouldn't. And if he didn't, Lulu's laughter said, that was his tough luck.

That was the last thing my mother gave me directly, gave me and meant to give: the unutterable conviction, on an afternoon when she was dying, that I was worthy of love.

3

I would give a great deal not to have needed that gift the way I did.

Around ten o'clock, I climbed the stairs and took the telephone up to the attic.

"Did you really miss my voice?" I asked Benjamin when he answered.

"Yes," he said. "I did."

"I'm glad."

"Is it very rough there?"

"Yes," I said.

"I never told you, but I thought your mother was wonderful."

"She's going to die."

"I know."

"You know?"

"I talked to Suzanne."

"The nurse," I said. "My predecessor."

"You didn't have a predecessor."

"That's sweet."

"She said once it reaches the liver—"

"I know. I miss you, Benjamin."

"I'll see you soon."

"When?" I asked, but he had already hung up.

4

I sat out on the porch the next day. Hillary was in with Lulu. Autumn was in the air already—cool breezes, a six o'clock sun at three. I had always loved autumn. I had always loved endings.

I closed my eyes. I listened to the creak of the rusted gate, which sounded like the birds' calls. There was the occasional hum of a plane or a motorboat, and the trees near the house scratching against the drainpipe when the breeze picked up.

I heard the plane approaching but was so drowsy that I didn't pay much attention until the noise was right on top of me, an urgent, overwhelming din that shook the planks of the deck. Hillary came running out of the house. I rushed to the edge of the porch with her. Benjamin's plane couldn't have been more than a hundred feet above us. I could even see his face. He made two passes at the house, waving a package out the window. He was wearing the sunglasses I'd given him, and he'd tied that silly aviator scarf to the right strut of the plane. On the third pass, he dropped the package as if it were a bomb. It hit the jetty, bounced into the water and bobbed there absurdly. Benjamin flew off. I looked at Hillary. The afternoon's stillness had returned.

"Go fetch," she said.

Hillary and I ran down the steps to the beach. She stood on the jetty, pointing to the small white package.

"This better be worth it," I said, and dove. The water felt icy and clean. I swam hard and straight, looking up every few moments to check that the package was still there. I was about twenty yards away when it began to sink.

"Jen!" Hillary was shouting. "Hurry!"

I dove under, opening my eyes. The package was sinking beneath me into the light green depths. I came to the surface, took a breath, plunged in again and managed to grab it.

Back on the beach, out of breath, I let Hillary open the package. It contained a soggy bouquet of daisies and yellow roses. Nothing more romantic has happened to me since. Attached was a note, just legible for all the water: "I'll be waiting for you at the Scavenger. Love, B."

5

I drove down Beach Street with the radio blaring and my hair still dripping wet. I thought: Benjamin loves me. I thought: Lulu will know that somebody loves me.

He was waiting inside the Scavenger. He was leaning against the jukebox, which was playing "String of Pearls." Another yellow rose was in his hand.

"How'd you get it to play that song on cue?" I asked.

"Simple," he said, not taking his eyes from my eyes. "I put in two dollars' worth of quarters and punched the button eight times."

"Really?"

"No."

"Oh."

"But I would have. I would have kept playing it till you came in."

I smiled and looked at my feet, the song bouncing around us. Benjamin touched my arm and offered me the rose. We walked outside, our footsteps crunching the pebbles in the driveway. We leaned against his car.

"What happened?" I asked him.

"I'm not sure, sweetheart."

"Lulu said I scared you. Did I scare you?"

"Yes."

"I didn't mean to."

"I know."

"It's a hard time."

"I know."

"When you love someone," I said, "you have to let them need you."

"Damn it," he said. "You're so damned sure."

"You must be too, or you wouldn't be here."

"Yesterday," he said.

"What happened yesterday?"

"I realized that if I let you go, I really might not get you back."

"That's right."

He stirred the pebbles with his foot.

"Can I get you back?" he asked.

I felt my throat tighten. I forced a laugh. "I think this is when I'm supposed to make you sweat," I said. "I think this is when you're supposed to make me cry."

"Let's not and say we did."

I laughed. He cupped my face in his hands and kissed me. "If it's all or nothing," he said, "I can't choose nothing."

6

We drove back to the house in tandem, Benjamin pulling up alongside my car whenever the road was wide enough. In the rearview mirror, my eyes danced like my father's.

Hillary was standing in the garden when the two of us drove up. She looked ill.

"How are you with wiring?" she asked Benjamin. Her voice sounded high and pinched.

"I majored in wiring at Yale," he said.

"Seriously."

"It depends."

"It's for Lulu," she said. "It's hard to hear her. I thought maybe we'd hook up a buzzer that she could press when she needed us. Maybe put a bell or something at each end of the house."

"Easy," he said.

"Really?" I asked him. "You could do that?"

"Nothing to it."

He got back into his car.

"I won't be long," he said, and then drove off in a cloud of dust. Hillary reached down for a rock and casually tossed it at a rabbit.

"He wants me back," I said.

"I figured."

"Oh, Hills."

She sat down on the grass.

"Isn't it hard for you," she asked slowly, "with Lulu like this now?"

"I think she's happy for me," I said.

"I guess."

I knelt beside her. The grass was dry. We hadn't been watering it enough.

"I wish," Hillary admitted, "I had someone."

"Call Spencer."

"No way." She laughed grimly, clutching her ankles, tossing her hair back. "Spencer is only for good times."

I went down to the beach to look for Daddy and saw him around the point, walking toward the house.

"I was just going to find you," I said. We sat down, side by side.

"Any change?"

"I don't think so. She's sleeping. Daddy? Benjamin wants me back."

"That's nice, darling. I'm glad. I am."

"He's going to hook up a buzzer for Lulu so we can hear her when she needs us."

"Good."

"Do you want to meet him, Daddy?"

"I met him. That morning at the airport."

"I mean really talk to him," I said.

"There'll be time."

"No there won't!"

He looked at me, surprised, his glasses throwing off crazy

light. "Of course there will, darling," he said. He picked up a handful of sand and spilled it out slowly.

"What is it?" I asked him.

"I did the strangest thing," he said.

"What, Daddy?"

"Last night. I'm almost embarrassed to say."

"Tell me."

He laughed, and lines I hadn't seen before appeared on his face in a thin gray web.

"I was walking around in the living room," he said. "Lulu was just in so much pain."

"Go on."

"Well, I went to the chessboard, and I looked at the figures, the king and queen—"

"Oh, Daddy."

"I picked up the timer, the hourglass, you know?"

"What did you do?" I asked softly, touching the back of his hand.

"I broke it," he said, looking up at me. "I took the damned thing in my hands and snapped it in two, right at the center, and the sand spilled out."

"Oh, Daddy."

"I'm going to get a drink. Want one?"

"All right."

We climbed the stairs to the house, but before we went in he stopped at the door.

"Do you think she was really happy?" he asked.

"Of course, Daddy. Of course she was."

"Do you think she had any regrets? Do you think she really wanted to go on painting?"

"You gave her what she wanted."

"I keep thinking."

"Don't think," I told him, and realized I meant it for the first time in my life.

7

"You're very sweet," I said to Benjamin when he came back from town. He sat at the dining room table, spreading out spools of wire and bells and buttons. He knew how things worked. I didn't. I had only managed it with the plane.

I heard the click of the bedroom door as Daddy closed it behind him.

"I'm going back to work," he said gruffly, walking into the dining room. I could tell that he'd been crying.

"Hello, sir," Benjamin said, leaping to his feet.

"Don't call me sir. It's Milo."

"Thanks."

"I don't suppose you could hook up one of those bells to reach the studio."

"It would take a lot of wire."

"I guess."

"Anyway, Daddy," I said, "you should work."

"That's right, Dad," Hillary said from the kitchen. "Lulu wants you to keep working."

"I wonder," he said, more to himself than to us.

"I'm sorry," I said to Benjamin after Daddy had gone out to the porch.

"For what?"

"For Daddy. That's not really Daddy."

"Don't be silly." He turned toward Hillary. "Why don't I tell you how to hook this up?"

"You do it," she said, much to my surprise.

"I wouldn't feel right," he said.

"It's okay. She'll just keep sleeping."

He looked at me warily.

"Really," I said. "She will. She does."

"Well, come with me, then," he said.

Softly we walked down the corridor. I was in love with his politeness, which was also, I think, what first won Hillary over. I turned the doorknob gently. We tiptoed in. Benjamin deftly leaned over Daddy's side of the bed, placing the buzzer by Lulu's hands. Thieflike, he ran the cord behind the headboard, around the dressers and back out the door. Lulu hadn't stirred. I stood and looked at her for a moment, half believing that she would wake up and be fine. I thought of all the Sunday mornings, with the four of us stretched across this bed. It occurred to me that there would be no new things to remember. The number of memories would become as finite as the memories themselves.

I think that afternoon was when we all started drinking. We drank gin and tonics, and vodka and tonics, and sometimes we drank straight Scotch. We couldn't get drunk, though, not even tipsy, not even just a little bit numb.

Beyond the glass doors the sunset was pale and pure, a single sun on the water like a stamp on wax.

8

At night, Benjamin and I made love. When we did I cried. I felt too much. I didn't know if it was love for him, or sadness for Daddy, or horror for Lulu. But a tightness was in my throat that even the crying didn't take away, and when I put my head against Benjamin's chest and he hugged me, he said, "I'm not going to leave you, sweetheart. I'll stay as long as you need me here."

I dreamed of Lulu dying. I saw her placed in a casket and lowered into the lawn. Daddy stood by a tree, carving their names into crumbling bark. The rabbits jumped and played in the bushes like light.

I woke with my arms around a pillow. It was still dark outside. Benjamin wasn't next to me. I looked up and saw him across the room, sitting at my desk.

"What are you doing over there?" I asked.

"Watching you."

"Why?"

"You weren't sleeping well."

"I'm sorry. I kept you up."

"It doesn't matter."

"Come back to bed. I'll give you a back rub."

"Don't be silly," he said.

We heard the buzzer ring.

"It works," I said.

"Should you go?"

"Let Hillary."

"Why don't you do it?"

"All right. I'll go."

I got out of bed and dizzily pulled on Benjamin's flannel shirt. On my way downstairs, the buzzer kept sounding. I wondered where Daddy was. The kitchen clock said three, and the light was on, and the dinner Hillary had made for him was still covered up on the stove, untouched.

"What is it, Lulu?" I asked, walking into her room. Daddy's side of the bed was still made.

"Bathroom," she mumbled.

"All right."

I pulled off her covers, turned her over and then reached to help her sit up.

"I don't know if you're going to be strong enough," she said.

"Of course I will," I said, wondering if I really would be. "Ready?" I asked.

"Not yet. I'm dizzy."

"We'll wait then," I said, trying to sound cheerful. I was still dizzy myself. My hands were cold. Then Lulu began to nod.

"Come on," I said. "Lulu. Come on. You're falling asleep."

I put her arm over my shoulder and, side by side with her, slowly stood her up. Her skin felt very odd to me—dry and soft and somehow new. Her lips were cracked, her smell was terrible, her stomach was so swollen that she looked pregnant. I led her into the bathroom, walking invalid steps beside her. I pulled her nightgown up around her and gently sat her down.

Then I started to leave.

"No. Stay," Lulu said.

I waited, embarrassed, perched on the sink. Lulu's hands were placed neatly before her, resting on her thighs. I thought of all the lovely poses that I'd seen her strike for Daddy. I thought of counting out the memories, assigning them numbers, dates, places, like all my strips of negatives.

"Lulu?" I asked her gently.

"Give me another minute."

"Want me to run some water?"

"Good idea."

Once, at my doctor's office, Lulu had told me to run some water and to think of the tide coming in on Sanders.

"Think of the tide coming in," I said to her.

I would sit on the blue bench with the stucco paint, and I would never see them again.

"I just can't do it," Lulu was saying.

"Let's get you back to bed."

"Damn," she said.

"Don't worry. I'm right upstairs," I said. "We can try again in a little while."

"All right."

I hopped off the sink and walked over to her, tucking my hands under her arms.

"Ready?" I asked, beginning to lift her.

"No—"

But I'd already started to pull her up. She rose no more than an inch or two. I put her back down.

"Oh, God," she said. She was scared, and I was too.

"Hey, Lulu," I said. "Don't worry. We've just got to get our timing right."

"I don't think you're strong enough. Where's Hillary?"

"Sure I am," I said.

We waited a few moments. I stroked her head and kissed the back of her neck. Then we tried again. At the moment I felt her falter, I strained as hard as I could to keep her up. I managed to hold on.

"See?" I said as we walked slowly back to her bed. "You thought I was a weakling."

"Never," she said, as I sat her down on the bed. "Not my own little girl."

I tucked her in and kissed her forehead.

"If you need me, I'm here," I said.

I climbed the stairs, shaky and tired. She had probably known I was afraid, I thought. Benjamin was back in bed. His arms closed around me as I lay down beside him.

"You okay?" he asked sleepily.

"I'm okay," I said, but my legs were shaking. He held me.

"You're a brave girl," he said. "And I love you very much."

I nestled beside him and let his body warm me. I was drifting off to sleep when the buzzer rang again.

"Oh God," I said.

"I wish I could help."

"So do I."

I don't know how Hillary slept through that night, or if she really did. In the end, I stopped counting the times I awakened to the sound of that horrible buzzer. Daddy still wasn't back, and I realized he had probably been through this every night and hadn't said a word about it. I finally stayed with Lulu, stretched out beside her until she fell asleep. I even sang her a lullaby, thinking if she were a real baby, fighting hunger instead of death, I would have done all the things I'd done that night but with none of the dread and panic.

9

In the morning, Daddy appeared in the kitchen as Benjamin and I were making breakfast. It didn't seem to register with him that Benjamin had stayed the night.

"Did you fall asleep out there?" I asked.

"I guess."

"Lulu had an awful time."

"I'm sorry, darling. Were you up with her?"

"Yes. Can I come see it yet?"

"No, darling," he said. "Not yet. Not quite yet."

"When are you going to show her?"

"I don't know."

He went into their bedroom.

Benjamin looked upset.

"Are you sure I'm not intruding?" he asked.

"I want you to be here," I said. He canceled his lessons and left to feed Rufus and pick up some clothes from his house. He was back by ten, and we spent the morning together, an isolated morning, an island like the one we were living on. Sunburned, sandy, we drank Bloody Marys and stayed sober.

At noon, Hillary came down to join us.

"We're going to fly her off the day after tomorrow," she said, "unless she's much worse tonight."

"Who said?"

"Daddy. He called Dr. Irving."

I dug my hands into the sand.

"I guess we'll stay and close up the house, right?" I asked.

"I guess," Hillary said.

"Is she sleeping now?"

"Yeah."

"She won't see Daddy's sculpture."

"I know," Hillary said.

"You want to swim?"

"Would you mind?"

"No. Go ahead. It's all right."

Benjamin and I climbed the stairs to my bedroom. He knew enough not to make love to me. I would lean into the cabin and kiss her good-bye. I took out a box of old photographs and showed him pictures of Lulu. Then I took out another stack of prints, and another. There was Lulu in Boston, on Sanders, Lulu with artists, dealers, with us as children, Lulu posing for Daddy, Lulu young, with long blond hair, Lulu older, staring straight at the camera, defiant, her chin raised, her face proud. Lulu and Daddy wading out of the ocean at dusk.

"She's very beautiful," Benjamin said.

"I wish you could have known her."

He went to take a shower and left me alone with my mother's life. I stared at the pictures until the images doubled and blurred. Downstairs in that bedroom was a woman who bore no resemblance to these photographs. I had frozen the past but could not make it dissolve again. I wanted it all to be over.

Hillary walked in and saw the photographs.

"How can you look at them?" she demanded, her towel falling away from her bathing suit.

I stared up at her, speechless.

"How can you?" she shouted. "How?" She swept the photographs off the bed in a furious rush. "This woman doesn't exist any more!" she cried. "She doesn't exist any more!"

Hillary ran from the room and down the stairs. She banged the screen door behind her. Then the buzzer sounded. No, I thought. No. I picked up the photographs one by one, stacking them on my desk. The buzzer sounded again. No. I lit a cigarette, my hands shaking, and sat at the desk. I listened to Benjamin humming in the shower. Five minutes must have passed. Then the buzzer rang a third time. I threw the cigarette on the floor and ground it into the beautiful wood with my sneaker. I went downstairs.

She was facing the door, her hands on her pillow, the buzzer near her head. Her eyes opened as I came in. She looked at me, a judge.

"What do you want?" I asked, trying to control the anger in my voice.

"Oh, Jen," she said slowly. "How could you."

"How could I what?" I asked.

"You know."

"No I don't."

"I rang."

"I'm here."

"I rang before."

"I didn't hear," I said.

With incredible effort, she turned away from me. "You're a liar," she said.

"No I'm not."

"You heard me."

"Maybe," I said, "maybe you only thought you rang."

There was a long silence.

"Out," she said. "I don't want you near me."

I started to run from the room, just as Hillary had upstairs. But we were as tied to her dying as to her love. A few moments later, we were both beside her.

10

Benjamin and I walked down to the stream. We sat on the bridge and hung our feet over.

"I wish she would die," he said. "I wish, for all your sakes, she would die."

The lake stretched out beyond the stream, black and still, like a slab of marble.

11

At night, I woke to the sound of Lulu retching downstairs.

"Oh God, oh God," I said.

"Sweetheart."

"They'll die. It's okay. They're going to die," I said.

"Not him. Don't be that way," Benjamin said.

"No." It would be the end of the summer.

"He's young. He'll be okay."

"I'm going to kill them," I said into the pillow. "They're both going to die." I would lean into the cabin and kiss them good-bye.

"Wake up, sweetheart," Benjamin said. "Sweetheart. Jennifer. Wake up. You're dreaming. You're having a nightmare."

I sat up slowly, so he'd know I was awake.

"Daddy said this year would never seem like anything but a nightmare."

He sat me up between his legs, my head resting on his

chest. "You were dreaming," he said. "You were having a bad dream."

"Benjamin," I said, talking to his hands, "when we were little and we went somewhere—you know how parents when they travel with their kids take two separate planes in case something happens?"

"We never went anywhere," he said, rocking me gently.

"Well, we did," I said.

He kept on rocking me.

"Lulu and Daddy never took separate flights," I said. "They wouldn't have *wanted* to go on without each other."

"I don't understand," he said, and the rocking stopped.

I pulled his arms around me like a shawl.

"I don't want him to live without her," I said. "He can't. He doesn't want to."

"He'll be all right."

I turned around.

"No he won't. Don't you see? Don't you see?"

"It'll take some time. It always does," he said. "But he'll get through. I did. And I didn't have you."

"Why don't you see what I'm saying? I'm not going to make him do it."

"You're exhausted, sweetheart," he said, sounding a little scared. I started to hate him. "You don't know what you're saying."

"Yes I do," I said. Lulu would have to be flown off the island. She would be transferred from our car to the back seats in the plane. Daddy would climb into the cockpit. I'd lean into the cabin and kiss her good-bye. I'd say:

"See you tomorrow. Just as soon as Hillary and I close up the house."

Then I'd kiss Daddy good-bye and whisper: "Call us if anything happens."

Then I'd walk back to the blue bench with the stucco paint, and I would feel very brave and certain, and I would wait while the plane took off, and Daddy would never have to be alone and I would never see them again.

"I'm going to go to sleep," I said to Benjamin.

"Good idea," he said.

But I stayed awake a long time, and I knew that he was awake still too.

12

When I woke in the morning, Benjamin was already dressed. He was sitting at my desk.

"Black or white," he said. "All or nothing."

"Both or neither," I said, not quite awake.

"Did you mean it?" he asked as I sat up in bed.

"What?"

"Did you mean it?"

I looked at him, eager, then terribly sad. After all that we'd done, he was scared of me.

"No," I said softly. "I didn't mean it." We would stay behind them to close up the house.

He stood up slowly, not at all sure, but wanting, I knew, to believe me.

"You love them too much to do something like that."

I wanted to make it clear to him: I loved them *so* much that I had to.

"I know" was what I said instead. "I was just upset. I had a bad dream."

I wanted him gone that moment. I would sit in the sun on the airport benches.

"Get dressed, sweetheart," he said. "Let's go for a walk, okay? Let's go for a walk."

Reluctantly, I got out of bed.

"Shouldn't you get to your lessons?" I asked as I pulled on my shorts and a turtleneck.

"I'll cancel them again," he said. He tried to hug me. I picked up a comb and pretended to fuss with my hair instead.

"Shouldn't you feed Rufus?" I asked him.

He sat down. "You want me to go," he said.

"I don't know."

"Let's go for a walk first."

"No," I said. I went into Hillary's room and out onto her porch. It was overcast and humid. Sea gulls circled the jetty and the shore and plunged, one by one, into the opaque water.

I wanted to cry and have Benjamin gone. I would sit on the benches and wave good-bye. I would never see them again.

"I love you," he said, whispering to my neck as he came up behind me.

"It's not you, sweetheart," I said. I strained to smile a smile that he would believe. "I just want to be with her today. I want to be with her."

I looked down at the railing of the porch until he had gone. Then I waited until the sound of his car faded. The waves came back like an old argument, lapping against no images, no silhouettes, bearing no horses to shore.

13

I wasn't thinking about what I would find in Daddy's studio. I only wanted to find him.

"Daddy," I cried, tugging open the door.

The room was dark. I turned on the light and stood, astonished and terrified. What I had last seen had been a half-dozen horses—a sad, lovely gesture, a final I love you. Now I was looking at sculpture. I was looking at Milo Burke. Before me was a whole carousel, brilliant and funny, exquisitely new. Not a gift, like her birthday box, but something that he could show, could have critics write about, could sign, could sell.

Everything but a roof was done. Ten horses, each on a brightly colored pole, formed a jaunty circle that reached the edges of the studio. I recognized Pillari and Bob. Daddy had painted an ocean on Bob's saddle and given him carved seashells for eyes. I saw a horse that I knew was Daddy. It was white with red trim and a brown, curly mane that looked like Daddy's hair. It had mournful eyes and its head was bowed. Its saddle was carved in the shape of an artist's palette, and its reins were suede, just like Daddy's old jacket.

Benjamin was a Pegasus—a horse with wings. He had a long, funny snout, an orange heart-shaped saddle and a pommel of three red roses. Then there was Dr. Irving, with a bushy, extravagant white mane. And Sam—undeniably Sam: he had a rigid back, and a body made from planks of four-inch-wide wood—the wood of our house's decks. Sam was trimmed in white, like the railings that Lulu had always asked him to paint.

I didn't recognize the others at first, but I knew that they had meaning, and they had life. They seemed to have just stopped moving when I walked in the door.

I wandered around the carousel, touching a head here, a mane there. I saw, for the first time, the centerpiece. I had read that in old-time carousels there had been calliopes in the center with three or four painted panels. Daddy had painted an ocean scene that stretched around the whole centerpiece: three frolicking blond sea nymphs: Lulu, Hillary and me.

But it was not about Lulu, this piece of art. She was not in it. Only he was.

It was a great piece of work. I knew even then, that day, that it would be Daddy's greatest. But Lulu wasn't in it. He had not done it for her.

I sat down on the edge of it and looked and looked for Lulu. My sadness turned to fury. I could not find her there.

I stayed for several hours, hoping that no one would come looking for me. I couldn't imagine facing Lulu, knowing that she had been left out.

14

"I saw it," I yelled up at Daddy. He was standing on the porch when I finally made my way back down the beach toward home. "I saw it," I said again, climbing up the stairs.

"You went in?"

"Benjamin left," I said. "He didn't understand. I needed to talk to you. I thought you'd be there."

He sighed. He tucked his hands in his pockets.

"Well, it isn't quite finished," he said.

"It's finished enough," I said bitterly.

"Almost."

"It's the best thing you've done," I said. But Daddy didn't seem to hear the accusation in my voice.

He smiled. "I'm very proud of it," he said.

"Why didn't you do this before?"

"I don't know."

"Why? Why did you do it *now?*"

"I really don't know, darling. I really don't know."

"Didn't you do it for her, Daddy?"

He thought. "Maybe I started that way."

My heart was racing. My hands were cold.

"Please," I whispered. "Tell me that you did it for her."

"You can't," he said after waiting a moment. "You can't do it for anyone."

"How could you do it at *all?*"

"Darling," he said to me. "I had to."

15

I stretched out beside Lulu that evening, an echo of her, a double image. I rubbed her back. I'm not sure that she could feel my hands. All she could say was my name.

I sang to her and watched the shadows move across the room. Drugged, a stranger, she wanted only to be. There was no *how* left to her life, nor to what she wanted from ours. There were no adjectives to give her—no beautiful, no talented, no loving, no special. All we could give her was a little bit of comfort, and the knowledge that we wanted her to live.

Hillary came and took over for me. Both of us were crying. I went to the beach and saw Daddy wading out of the ocean alone.

A bonfire blazed down the beach at a neighbor's house, and I saw a pale moon rise above my father like a small white lie.

"I *had* to," he'd said. Had to, I thought.

16

It was just past midnight when I left for the airport.

"I have to get out of here, just for a while," I told Hillary.

"Be back when you can," she said.

I drove with the taillights before me blurring.

At the airport, a single beacon from the tower swept the fields. But the lights were off in the terminal, and no one was around. Slowly I walked across the grass to Daddy's plane. I stared down at the hinges of the tail. I picked up one flap. I moved it up and down and watched it, under the eerie light of the beacon, as it disengaged from the hinge and broke off in my hand. I threw it on the grass. It was beyond fixing.

I sank down next to the plane and watched the beacon as it crossed my legs every few seconds. Off and on, dark and light, black and white. I was half me and half invisible. The particular pain I'd planned on had vanished, and the truth lacked everything the pain had had: romance, strength, control. Suddenly I was just another child about to lose her mother. Her death seemed the dark side of the beacon. I ran to the car.

17

I called Benjamin in the morning.

"You were right," I said. "I couldn't do it."

"I don't understand," he said.

"You don't really need to. But you have to fly my parents to Boston today."

"Why?"

"Because I couldn't do it."

"I don't understand," he said again.

"You don't *have* to."

There was a long, difficult silence. Then he said: "Did you do something to his plane?"

"Yes," I said.

Benjamin sighed and then cursed.

"Will you fly them home?" I asked him.

"Yes."

"We'll be there at three."

18

"You'll want to take care of Lulu," I said to Daddy. "You won't want to have your mind on flying."

They were the first words I'd spoken to him since the day before. He agreed to let Benjamin do the flying.

As he and Hillary packed for Lulu and got her dressed and ready, I went to the garage. I found the ax that Sam used to chop firewood. Shielding it with my body, I walked down to the beach.

19

Daddy had locked the studio door. I swung the ax and was surprised by its weight. The head stuck in the door. I pried it loose and swung again, and the thin plywood gave way. I reached my hand into the hole I had made and turned the doorknob from inside. I opened the door and stepped inside. In the darkness, the horses seemed to grin.

I walked around the room, taking down Daddy's drawings from the walls, stacking them neatly on his worktable, finding a brick to weight them down. Then I climbed up onto the horse that was Daddy. The canvas roof ripped easily. Light came in. I saw the sky and heard the ocean. I widened the slit with the ax and pulled down. The canvas fell like a curtain. The rest of it tore easily when I reached up with my hands and pulled. I jumped down from the horse and walked around the carousel, gathering up the dark heavy cloth and stashing it in a corner. Then I was ready. I picked up the ax again and swung at the corner of the wall. I swung again. I aimed for the spot I had just hit and swung a third time. A thin crack appeared. I went to the other corner and swung three times there. Then I rested, leaning on the ax handle. My hands were already feeling raw.

Then I swung at the middle of the wall. A sliver of light appeared in the right-hand corner. I heard a loud crack. I swung again. A few more heavy blows, and the whole wall fell—slowly, wonderfully, hitting the dirt with a muffled thud. After the second wall, the others seemed easy. Finally, I stood with all four walls down around me like a flower that had opened.

20

Hillary and I half-carried Lulu to the car. She had not been outside for days, and although she felt terrible, she paused for a moment before letting us help her into the car. She looked around her lawn and raised her chin.

We drove down the dirt road, Daddy at the wheel, Hillary beside him, Lulu next to me in back. As we neared the bridge, we could see bits of color through the trees that looked like painted leaves. Daddy slowed the car down.

"Oh my God," he said.

"Don't be mad," I whispered.

"Kid," Lulu said, blinking, confused.

Daddy stopped the car a few yards from the carousel. No one moved. We all stared. I looked at Lulu's face.

"Daddy painted you on the center," I told her.

The horses seemed to prance in the lush woods. Lulu reached for Daddy's hand and gripped it. He kissed hers very gently.

"Oh, kid," she said again, smiling now. "I want to get out and see it."

"Benjamin's waiting for us," Daddy said. He turned back to the wheel and said, "You can always see it in Boston."

Lulu leaned back. "Of course," she said. "I'll see it there."

After a few moments, he started the car again. The road curved down to the beach. Lulu had shut her eyes. Hillary was crying.

"Tree," Lulu said, the sunlight flickering across her face.

Daddy met my eyes in the mirror. I shook my head back at him.

"Jen," he hissed.

"I can't," I whispered.

"Jen."

"Carousel," I said, looking at Lulu.

"Wrong," she said, her eyes still closed. "Milo," she said. She could have just been saying his name. But I think she knew about that sculpture what I'd taken the whole summer to find out, and at last be grateful for.

21

At the airport Lulu said to Daddy: "You be the grown-up today."

I could see Hillary frantically wiping the tears from her face, still trying hard to pretend.

It was the end of the summer. We were wearing sweaters and slacks. Bright yellow goldenrod was growing on the sides of the roads. The sky was deep blue.

Benjamin was at the plane. He was calm and efficient, and he helped Lulu climb in. Daddy took the copilot's seat. I leaned into the cabin. Lulu's eyes were shut tight, but she smiled when I kissed her good-bye.

"See you tomorrow," I said, "just as soon as we close up the house."

Then I kissed Daddy good-bye. "I'll have Sam start crating it up," I said.

He nodded. "Thank you," he said.

"Call us if anything happens. Even if you just want to talk."

I looked at Benjamin. He did not look back. I thanked him quietly and walked back to the blue bench with the stucco paint, and I waited as Hillary said her good-byes. I made us stay while the plane took off. I watched until the small yellow spot dissolved into the sky, and I realized that I would see them again the next day.